The Krewe

Herbert and Melancon Book Number One

By
Seth Pevey

1

When you run over a human being with a train, there isn't so much as a bump for those people riding or conducting inside the cars themselves. People are just too soft, and trains too hard and inestimably heavy. It might as well be mud under the flanged steel.

But there didn't need to be any physical sensation for the conductor, 47-year-old James LeBlanc, to know that he had indeed cut a man in two. Probably three or four pieces really, but he hadn't been able to bring himself to look at the aftermath of what he had done— or what the train had done, anyway.

The dissected man had never screamed, James the conductor believed that. Immediately after the body disappeared beneath the wheels, James had hardened himself and listened well. He tried to block out the train sounds as only a conductor could, cringing in that expectation. The waiting had seemed to stretch out as he hearkened for any human sound, a wail or yelp, but there was nothing.

It must be instant, James thought, *it must feel like nothing to be run over by a train*. Then in that moment, and for years after, he repeated it to himself often.

But the fact of the matter was that a man had died, "had come out of the fog," as he explained it. "A man where a man shouldn't be. Out of the cypress trees there along the river. The willow logs and the duck pools. Out of nowheres. One minute there was nothing at all, and the next there he was, long arms and wide shoulders, kneeling there on the tracks and facing away from the train."

"Away?"

"Yes, away."

In that hot instance James the conductor had known the full futility of applying any brakes to the situation, but he'd done so anyway. It was policy of course, and there would be questions. You did not cleave a man like that, even a man that seemed to figure on being chopped up, without a lot of papers, and questions, and old men in out-of-fashion suits leveling their challenging eyes at you over those desks that always seemed to shine a tad bit too brightly. So, in that moment, as James explained it, he'd applied the brakes and listened hard for that last cry of a dead or dying man, telling himself that it was surely only a brief snap before darkness. *Just like falling asleep.* He'd applied the brakes and waited and what the hell else is there to say about it?

James knew what he'd seen and felt. But it wasn't that easy. Later he would drink. He would cry, drunk, during commercial breaks. Later he would see the man's back in his closet, kneeling away from him in the darkness as he went in to find fresh socks or his box of old letters. James could not have told these things to the detective though, even had he known them. It was the facts that were important now. A man was dead.

"No the man did not cry out. I believe I've been plenty clear on that," James told the police detective.

"Was there any noise at all?"

"I'm sorry, I thought I'd explained all this?" James was shivering, the train-trembling in his bones that never seemed to dissipate, and that damn shine on the detective's table. The look in his eyes.

Detective Melancon was old and thin. His clothes fitted poorly and were of a forgotten color. But his eyes were bright, pale blue, piercing, and his mouth seemed far from tired. He cleared his throat and sat down.

"You know, James. The human mind is a terrible, awful recording device. For starters, it remembers things plain

3

wrong more often than not. Emotion clouds the mechanism, you see. Even the brain of a sharp man like yourself. You're an engineer, right? So, do me this favor. Forget for a second about the dead guy. Just explain this to me like you were explaining the workings of…say a combustion engine. Cold and practical, just like that. I know you must be upset, running over a fella and all. But I need to hear it all a couple times. It's always better hearing a story a few times. I find it helps for…clarity. Now James, I need you to be clear. Think hard. What else did you see?"

"I didn't run over him. The train did," James replied.

There was a long pause. "Sure, I know that James."

James softened in his chair. "He looked fit. Tall, big like maybe a football player or something. The way he was kneeling was almost kind of regal."

"Regal?"

James fidgeted. "I don't know. Like, a guy about to get knighted in one of those old stories. Two hands across his knee you know. Kneeling down. A quarterback posing for his picture."

The detective ran his fingers through the little swirl of blonde hair dusting the top of his head. He rubbed his eyes and then his temples.

"And you say he didn't react. He just knelt there, facing away from you? No last-minute hesitation or jerking, anything like that?"

"No. Nothing at all. It looked like he was just waiting for the thing to be over," James said. He thought he might have a small inkling of what the dead man must have felt, sitting here with the detective and wanting a drink so bad he could weep, waiting patiently for destiny to crest so that it might crash down on his head. There was a lot of waiting left to do. Nervous, restless waiting. Life was made of waiting. Waiting for the train to load, waiting to arrive, waiting for the blood and guts to be cleaned from the wheels so you could get the shipping containers into port. Perhaps death was all waiting as well. Whatever might come of this particular incident, it was going to be an awful long wait for it to all go away. An awful long time for him to chug along under the weight of it all. Him that had done nothing but his job.

"James the conductor...you are a human being," the detective said, as if to himself. "A distraught human being, having a conscience nagging at him and what not. This is to be expected. And perhaps as a...distraught human being, you have failed to notice and recall some small particulars, some tiny details. It was late and the air had held that swampy texture that...you know...sometimes keeps secrets."

There was a long and heavy pause filled with that look again. The detective just kept talking.

"Swamp gas, it makes people see ghosts and UFOs sometimes. But what does it matter really? You don't go down to the riverside train tracks, on a school night no less, and kneel before an oncoming locomotive. Not unless you want that sweet hereafter. At least that's how James the conductor sees it…am I getting close here friend?"

James blew out air. He looked from side to side, seeking succor on the cinderblock walls. It felt like talking about sex with a priest somehow.

"Detective, honest to God what the hell does it matter how I see it? I flip a lever, the train goes. I hit the brakes, it stops a few football fields down the way. Now, I don't know what else you want me to say. I told you, all of it took about 3 seconds. I saw him. I applied the brake. And then we just went over him you know?"

Melancon rubbed his head. He stood up, began pacing across the room, stopped before a filing cabinet at the far end by the door. James was wondering what bullshit form he would have to fill out, only to be surprised when Melancon pulled a bottle out from the beige wasteland of the cabinet. Two glasses followed and the drawer slid shut on its tracks with a grinding, metallic finality that dropped James' tremble into a lower gear.

"You're a drinker, aren't you?" Melancon asked.

"I don't drink on the job, if that's what you're asking."

"Oh, of course not. I assume they probably already put you through a drug test as well."

"Yeah...something like that."

"So drink up."

James watched the amber liquid fall into the glass. There had been no sound as the man's bones had cleaved apart. No sound as he was sucked under into the hell that exists under a train. But the sound of that liquid falling in that glass was thunderous.

"Why would you choose that?" James blurted out, transfixed on the tumbler.

"Excuse me? It happens to be a very fine scotch."

"No, I mean... Why would you want to die that way?"

The detective's body bobbed. He held up his scotch and then crossed his arms. James, while terribly thirsty, thought that this guy needed a shave, needed to talk and smile less, and definitely didn't need to pour drinks. He was too open and familiar already without the booze lubricating the wheels any more. But then, maybe that was the way they got you to talk. They lubed you until you became like a runaway freight rolling down the hill towards a stalled school bus full of children and nuns. Or long-limbed depressives kneeling by the dozen.

He needed to talk. But slamming the gate shut was a smarter track. He'd have hard work to do at home but now was no time for going off the rails.

"Well, it's like this Jimmy. May I call you that? Sometimes suicides don't just want to *die*. They also sometimes want to *feel* the pain." He took a long sip of his drink and leaned across the desk. "You know, just like how the bite of whiskey is a sort of… pleasant pain…reminds you that you are still… alive…damnedest thing. Maybe they hate themselves. I don't know. Ever been suicidal Jimmy?"

The body language of the detective was casual and loose, but his blue eyes were not. They watched James minutely, measuring him.

James poured himself a second shot from the bottle and said:

"No, I never was suicidal, and I'm not now if that's what you're asking."

Melancon slapped him on the back. "You're salt of the earth Jimmy. I'm glad to get to know you, even under these circumstances."

"Going back to what you said before though, about feeling pain. You *do* reckon he felt pain then?"

The detective's face took on a thoughtful scrunch. "I don't know that I really thought about it that hard Jimmy, for obvious reasons. What do you reckon it feels like?"

James didn't answer.

The detective swirled his drink and downed it, smacking his lips. "I doubt it feels like a shiatsu massage, anyway."

James the conductor nodded somberly. "So, a suicide then, is that how you are putting this down on the books?"

The detective's eyes fell as he put the bottle away.

"We'll have to see Jimmy. Anyway, you are free to take off. You've got my card. Sometimes it's funny how it happens, but something might just pop into your mind. When that happens, give me a call."

James finally got up and walked to the door, stopped at the threshold and turned to look back at the detective.

"I just wonder who he was, is all."

2

"Man, you cut onions like old people fuck."

It was painfully true. Felix Herbert could barely use a knife. But he was trying anyway— focusing, sweating over the pearly spheres with tight teeth and a grip that was wildly inappropriate for the task.

But of course, Sweets, the provocative pastry chef, was like the rest of the *real* world, in that he just didn't care about a person's effort all that much. While Felix was slowly coming around to this and other facts, there were to be many growing pains. The spectacle of his hard-fought battle with the onion was just one of many.

"Gotta take your time to do it right, I guess," Felix mumbled. No one heard it.

"Man," Sweets continued, "you know you shit at this job Felix. My lil baby cousin got better knife work than your sorry ass."

Felix bunched up his lips, put down the knife and looked at Sweets in the eyes.

"I don't see you cutting any."

Sweets leaned his head back and raised his hands up in the air.

"Listen to this shit. Chopping ain't my job son. My job is cakes and pies and salads and all that cold and creamy bullshit. That's why I'm over there where it ain't 150 degrees." He pointed. "You the one over here sweating in all the food and shit. Salty ass."

Felix was a young man with long legs and wide shoulders, and he didn't seem to belong. Every metal edge, red-hot flame, hissing vent, and ex-con employee of this kitchen ran counter to the softness in his face, the leisure of his gait, the unearned angle of his chin. The rest of them knew it. They smelled it on him.

The dishwasher and the sous-chef both sat by the outside door to the kitchen, chuckling their smoke out into the night. Felix tried to bite his tongue and went back to work: lined up the blade carefully, perpendicular to the onion's grain, and let the weight of it carry down through the acrid, white flesh. It was a sharp knife, brand new, and he'd cut himself too many times.

It was hell being laughed at, but he understood it. He was younger than them, less experienced with hard work than they were. He certainly hadn't been to prison like at least two of them had, and wouldn't know the first thing about knife work if he hadn't come here on what increasingly felt like a foolish whim. He fought to keep the color from his cheeks.

The onion acid burned his eyes, and the heat lamps did, in fact, cause him to sweat into the food. It was inevitable. Just like it was inevitable that these three hard men were going to be giving him more of this throughout the shift— that men like these would be at him his whole life if he didn't learn to handle a knife, a hammer, a wrench the right way, and soon.

"You a cook right? So how did you even get to be a *cook*…. without knowing how to cook?" Sweets asked. "More importantly, *why* is you a cook? You got that look like you used to buying thousand dollar watches and shit."

Sweets did an unflattering walking impression then, all stiff and rigid. His performance was well received.

"Do you see me wearing any thousand-dollar watch?" Felix asked.

"Nah man, you probably didn't wear it cause you think we'd steal it."

It was Felix who now laughed, bent his head down. He slid the knife across the table and spit into the trashcan. Something came over him.

"I bet I can cut more onions in five minutes than you can. 100 bucks."

That took the smirk off of Sweets' face. He looked at Felix— that wide-eyed, rhetorical look of a workman.

"You fucking with me?" he said, cocking his head. He was paying attention.

Felix knew he'd lose as soon as he said it. Why had he said it then? Maybe just to derail the whole "make fun of Felix" train. Or, maybe, was it that he was trying to buy his way into some friendliness? He didn't know what he had in mind, but after saying it he was sure of one thing: now they were going to have his pride and his money in one easy swoop, and he'd only just been there a week.

And so, the onion chopping contest took place during a busy dinner rush. Fortunately for sporting sake, the executive chef who "ran" the kitchen was out in his wine bottle somewhere. So, the patrons wouldn't get their veal cutlets or osso bucco on time.

There were more important things at stake now.

The sous-chef stood holding his cell phone stopwatch aloft. Two plastic cutting boards were laid out side by side. Sweets ran his knife along an oiled whetstone and bobbed his head to the radio.

"On three," the dishwasher called over the printer, which rolled out a long ribbon of tickets that had now begun to droop to the floor unattended.

"Three, two, one, chop."

Sweets had a fine technique. He was left handed, and so used the knuckle of his right hand to guide the base of the blade as it rhythmically tapped through the onion. He had a way of letting his wrist go fluid, so that the turning of the knife landed like a wave through the vegetable. It was the kind of skill that was won through the absolute necessity of being useful. Felix knew this, knew all this in the space of one sigh, gaping at the man's fluttering, skillful hands— like old blackbirds, rough looking though fine in flight, delicate and calloused.

Sweet's half gallon bucket was halfway full before Felix could make it through the first onion.

He'd need to speed up. Not to win. Winning was impossible. However, he hadn't figured that he would be beaten in quite such a humiliating way. A degree of disgrace now seemed to be hanging in the balance. His slices were too measured and hesitant, and he kept turning his head to watch the flurry of competitive, artistic dicing happening just to his right.

By the time the fry cook began the countdown, Sweets had stopped chopping. His bucket full, he slipped his long and tattooed body up onto the metal countertop and was twirling the cutting board on his pointer finger like a basketball. The ticket machine kept rolling, and Felix didn't pause or break his small momentum. Instead he sped up. Perhaps an attempt to save a little face, or the simple knowledge that all of the onions had to be chopped anyway— but he kept chopping, all the way down to the "One" of the countdown, at which point his brain attempted to cut faster than his clumsy hands could follow, and the knife slipped. He sliced the meaty part of his left thumb nearly down to the bone.

He didn't cry out, but the other kitchen hands saw the blood and stopped laughing.

"Yo, Felix man. That's going to need stitches bruh."

He stood there with his kitchen towel wrapped around the pulsating muscle, the blood already soaking through and dripping down onto his apron and the grease mats along the floor.

"I still want my hundred bucks, but look, you going to have to carry your ass home or to the doctor or some shit. You can't be bleeding everywhere in these folk's food. Even with that blue blood."

But Felix didn't want to go home: it wasn't much of a place to go at the moment. All stacked boxes and paperwork and boredom. There'd be nothing for him there except for beige carpet, unpacked cardboard, jigsaw puzzles.

If not home then where? He certainly wasn't going to the doctor for a cut like this. Lately, he'd developed a slight distrust of the medical profession after hearing so many of his brother's horror stories, and a trip to the emergency room would make him feel even guiltier and sillier and more spoiled and useless than he already felt— sitting in there for two hours, among the people with their real problems, their gunshot wounds and ODs and their life-altering traumas.

Instead, Felix did what he always had done in such instances. He self-medicated.

It was quiet out in the main dining area. But the few seated patrons looked impatient. Crossed arms, side to side glances, the smell of wine. It wasn't well-lit, but the music was alright and the food, when it came, was good enough to keep those lights on.

Ducking into the restaurant's only bathroom, Felix locked the door. He had brought a Dixie cup full of cooking brandy and three of his large, blue, hydrocodone pills. Vicodin for the cut, for the shame of uselessness, for the boredom, for other invisible shortcomings he wouldn't have been able to name. Laying them flat in his good palm, Felix caught an unsavory glance of himself in the mirror. The sink was red with his blood, he was white-faced and harried and shining with grease. He looked away and threw the little flakes of happiness into his mouth, chewed them and then gargled the brandy to wash down the foul-tasting powder. Then he pulled a roll of duct tape out from below the sink, taped a few paper towels over his bleeding wound, covered the whole mess with a latex glove, and resolved within himself to feel and do better.

Then, just like that, the self-doctoring was over. Again, he looked in the mirror, his head hovering over the bowl of potpourri just barely detectable over the bleach he'd used, only six hours before, to clean the painted cement floor of the lavatory. Felix Herbert, with a buzz already coming along like warm honey in the pit of his stomach, looked at himself too long, trying to think about nothing, until a knock at the door broke his concentration.

"Yo, Felix."

It was Sweets.

"Yeah, I'll be back in just a second, and I'll write you a check. A check is good, right?"

"No man, listen. *Them people* is here and they asking for *you*. What the fuck you do bruh?"

"Them people?"

"Yeah. You know, the po-lice man."

Felix's pulse quickened, and now he looked in the mirror for a much different reason. It could all be a cruel joke, sure, but what if it were not?

Yes, dilated pupils. Yes, glaze over his green eyes. Yes, dark hair disheveled. Blood on his apron. One look would be all it took to guarantee incarceration, internet headlines going viral about the downfall of a well-to-do "black sheep" who was more sheepish than black, having yet to do anything either infamous or rebellious aside from getting this dumbass job.

But he felt good anyway in that temporary glow, and went through a lightning round of resignation followed by fatalism followed by anger and finally by excitement that at the very least, *something* was about to happen. He put himself into the future, thinking of all the headline possibilities.

"Loser Son of Pork Baron Sent to Pill-ory After Ill-advised Onion Bet."

He peeked out into the main dining room. Standing at the bar was a densely-built man in an NOPD uniform. His forearms were covered in tribal tattoos, and he was gym-muscled, crew-cut. He was chatting with the good-looking bartender Shelia. Felix trembled in his squishy kitchen clogs. Maybe he could outrun the guy?

"High speed Chase with Intoxicated Kitchen Hand Ends in Fiery Uptown Disaster."

The thoughts raced through his mind. What *had* he done? What could it possibly be? It could only be the drugs, right? Some pill bottle had fallen out of his backpack on the road and they had traced it here, to him. Do policemen usually come like this and haul you out kicking and screaming for a bottle of pain-pills? Who would he use his "one call" on? Did they still do that?

There was only one thing to do. Time to face the music. He walked out to the bar with his head held high.

"Felix Herbert?" the cop asked, and he took his hat off. It was that motion, the taking off of the hat, which disrupted Felix's whole chain of thought.

"Fry Cook Gets Terrible News," the headline now read.

"Let's talk outside," the cop said, and gave a nod to Shelia at the bar. She smiled but the officer didn't.

Outside the wind was ripping into the crepe myrtle branches, none of which had trusted the unusually warm February enough to bloom. The cop tucked his hat under his arm and pulled out a small note pad. He looked at Felix, then at the pad, then at Felix, then at the pad.

"You are Mr. Herbert, correct?"

Felix looked at the ground and told him that his name was indeed Herbert.

"Brother to Robert Herbert."

"Yes."

"Well. There is no way to say this that will help anything. So I'll just go ahead and say it. Young man, I'm sorry to inform you that your brother is dead. He was hit by a train."

Chapter 3

Felix stared back at the officer with a blank face, a slight quiver. His mind had heard the words, sure enough, but could issue no orders other than to simply stand there in front of the large window of the restaurant with staff and customers watching, wondering, and filling in blanks. He shook in the balmy air, blood still filling the latex glove he had slipped over his knife wound. The officer shuffled awkwardly and looked inside the restaurant with a kind of longing. He then gestured as if he would put a hand on Felix's shoulder but seemed to hesitate, and then abandon the idea.

"A train, but...how?"

"It looks like a suicide, son. You'll get all the details at a later time."

Felix continued to stare. This made the officer show a blush— a dark navy uniform and cherry red cheeks.

"Do you need a ride somewhere, son?"

"No, I think I'll walk."

The officer didn't seem to like that idea. "Are you sure you're ok? You look like you might need to sit down a minute."

"No no. Thanks. I'm alright. Just going to...going to walk home now I suppose."

The officer watched him.

"You should be with your family now," the cop said.

"Yeah...with family." Felix felt himself start to drift, a dreamy state overcoming him. He backed away, the police officer's face receding into the darkness. He found himself walking, a wave of nausea creeping up on him that tasted like awful cooking brandy and regret, deep in the pit of his stomach.

Out under the crepe myrtles of Palmer Street, the weight of it came crashing in. He looked all the way down to the wide avenue where the streetcar was just then grinding its way downtown. Death. Blood. Eternity. He could feel them in his chest, and the air was too thick to breathe.

Brother.

Felix had an image then of Robert twisting beneath a train. The sharp pain went from his stomach to his heart, but he put one foot forward and managed to make it over a root-mangled bit of sidewalk, and on to the next block and then the next, plodding on like a zombie until he arrived at his apartment complex by the river.

It was just as he would have expected, had he had time to do any expecting. The Continental sat idling by the curb, looking out of place, and telling Felix that his mother certainly already knew about Robert, that she'd not been shocked to torpor as Felix himself was, that she had the presence of mind to make at least this one arrangement.

"Master Felix," said a familiar and sad voice.

Tomás. The old man still had his wan smile. It had been a month and Felix had missed him terribly, though he hadn't realized how much until this very moment, and it took some of the bite out.

"I'm glad to see you, old man," Felix blurted.

Tomás the driver, the cook, the gardener, the raiser of sons, put his hand on Felix's shoulder and guided him into the backseat of the Continental.

"How long have you been waiting?" Felix asked.

Sliding into the driver's seat, Tomás pulled at his seat belt.

"No matter. I would sit here and wait for a long time if it meant bringing you to home with me. We have been trying to reach you, Felix. Madame informs me that your cellular phone has been dead. She's been very strong. She needs you now, and you need, I think, your phone. Wouldn't you like to charge it up front?"

"Sure, but I don't think I'll be turning it on just now."

Tomás seemed to think about this, peering into the rear-view mirror at his charge.

"You don't worry now. Let me know if I can do anything, Felix. Anything at all."

He started the car.

"Your eyes don't look so well Felix. Have you been crying?"

"You aren't going to say anything about Robert?" The words came out of Felix before he could stop himself. He choked on them, a tear pushing its way out of the corner of his eye.

"Sir," Tomás said.

"I'm sorry Tomás. I'm an asshole. And I'm high as a kite right now and I sure as hell don't know how to use a kitchen knife. My brother...my poor brother."

"You're just in the shock sir. Let's be quiet and listen to a soft song."

"Take me to them, then. And let's not listen to music Tomás. I missed you. Tell me about happy things in your life."

And Tomás did. He talked about the sunny weather. About the Saints almost making the playoffs. About the tomatoes in the garden. About a trip back home to Guatemala he'd been perennially planning but never seeming to take. He talked and talked until Felix had begun to come down to earth again, and at last they arrived at their destination.

Felix looked at his family house from the back seat, through the dark tinted windows of the Continental. The Christmas lights at 1066 St. Charles Avenue were never allowed to linger. In fact, all decorations were put up and taken down in a fastidious fashion that had always amazed him. It was the same with every blade of grass, every hedge, and every nest that any bug, squirrel, or bird was brazen enough to attempt construction of in the oak boughs that canopied the century-old manor. It was, as it had always been, a testament to the human penchant for control. But the enormous task that was the removal of the New Year's décor, and its replacement with the purple, gold, and green accoutrement of the Carnival season, had now been allowed to halt in an abortive, half-baked state on this evening. And it was a shock to see the place in such unfamiliar disarray.

Felix had grown up there, but he still felt a tad chilly at the prospect of going inside.

"Your…ahem… apron, Master Felix?"

He was still wearing the soiled kitchen apron, smeared with blood and grease. Still reeking of onion. The latex glove was now swampy and heavy with his blood, lolling at his side.

"Yeah, of course."

As they entered the side door, Tomás began to untie the apron from the back in an intimate gesture, a maneuver which he stopped suddenly when the clack of expensive shoes struck through that antechamber.

"My dear, sweet Felix," she said, when she saw that final son. She held him by the shoulders and looked at him sadly. After a few deep breaths and a long shake of the head, she released him and turned back towards the living room.

The two men followed.

"Hey, mama," he said. As he moved to the couch he felt the sudden urge to run and embrace her, but stopped short. She sat on the reading chair and put a hand to her mouth. He'd never seen her cry, and she didn't start now.

"He's dead?" Felix asked, shakiness coming into his voice again. The house echoed. The carpentry of restraint that dictated this great and empty place threw the words back at him. Maybe Felix would cry anyway. He almost decided to cry, right then and there. Should he cry? Was it allowed?

The pills and the booze and his inability to hug his own mother all worked on him, drawing him towards release.

She walked over and put her hand on his arm, sat down next to him, smiled at him as she had when he was younger. But there was pain now, new wrinkles and lines, whole volumes of lonesome hurt written in her squint.

Tomás left and returned with Felix's father. When placed near the fireplace in his wheelchair, facing the family, the old man's hoary head tilted towards some invisible pole in the inestimable distance, and stayed there. He did not look at Felix.

"Did Dad say anything, when you told him?" Felix asked his mother.

"No," she said. "He didn't say anything."

Felix walked over and stood under his father's gaze.

"Hey Pop, how are things?"

"Anna Karenina, she went under a train. You know that story? Morbid bunch, Russians. Too cold…too cold. I prefer the French for affairs of the heart."

His mother ignored the exchange, bid Tomás to fix her a Manhattan and then looked away, out of the window.

"He isn't going to understand this I think. It is almost as though I should be jealous of him," she said. "Of course we've cancelled all our plans. There is a lot to do now. I haven't even spoken to Angelica. Dear God, and those kids."

She crossed her arms and held herself stiff. Tomás appeared from the kitchen with the Manhattan on a silver tray.

"They said it was a suicide mother. A suicide."

She huffed.

"The Thane of Cawdor thought the trees would never come," Dad mumbled to himself in the corner, "CURSES, CURSES I SAY."

"When was the last time you talked to him Mother?"

"Just two days ago I went to his talk on, oh what was it? You know, on neuropathy or some such thing. I didn't understand a word, of course, but it was clear from the room that he was brilliant. You know how brilliant he was Felix. Everyone there loved it. I was so proud."

It looked as though she would begin sobbing. She hung there, on the edge of something terrible, a tremor of grief perhaps. She touched her hand to her breast. Her lips tightened but she only cleared her throat and took another

27

drink, turned away from him and faced the bay window looking out into the dark back lawn.

Tomás had crept in between them, his hands folded behind his back, waiting for the conversation to finish. He cleared his throat and announced: "it's the coroner Madame. They'd wanted to know if you would identify the body. I told them not to be ridiculous, that you couldn't be expected to…"

"Get my jacket, please Tomás."

Felix shook his head and sat down on the hearth, no intention of going to see any mangled, familiar corpses. His mother was stronger than him— strongest in the family now that Robert was gone. He knew it. They all knew it. Felix's father watched his spot on the wall with great intensity, knowing it all too somehow.

"Do you need any money, Felix?" his mother asked. It was often the last thing she said to him as they were parting.

"No. I'm fine." Which is what he had been trying to say, of late.

His mother gone, he sat there for three hours, during which time he went into his parent's bathroom cabinet and helped himself to two more pain pills. Money was one thing. At least, that is what he told himself as he downed the blue, oblong pills. For another twenty minutes, he sat with his father, listening, trying to parse the outbursts into some profundity of comfort, grief, love. All he recognized, and then only on occasion, were snippets of dialog, characters, plot points and settings. Most of the references were lost on him. Felix had never been a reader near the caliber of his father. No one was, really. And now it was all that was left of the old man's mind— pages and pages scrambled beyond repair.

There was a fine sunken cypress table in the parlor that held most of the family photographs. In the late hour Felix picked up a picture of his brother, walked back to the fire, and held it and its metal frame in his lap. A stranger might not have known that it was Robert pictured there. His eyes were masked and he sat high on horseback. It was the year he had been Champion of his first carnival Krewe, though Felix couldn't remember which. In the photograph, Robert wore a plastic Spartan helmet, comically oversized and with golden push broom bristles sticking out of the top. His horse was jet black and wore a covering that read "Bucephalus" in big Roman style lettering. Felix wondered if the javelin his brother carried in the picture was real, how sharp it might have been, how heavy, or if his brother had taken a few practice throws in the back yard before the parade started. It was a minor Krewe, but it was the one that had started his brother's lifelong obsession with Carnival flair and decorum.

"He was a happy person," Felix said into the fireplace. "Happy in a way that I've never been able to understand."

"Sanity and happiness are an impossible combination. That was Mark Twain. Mark Twain. Mark Twain. Two fathoms. Two fathoms. Full fathoms five thy father lies."

Felix smiled at his father. "Maybe you are right Dad."

"Might makes right, not two wrongs. Two wrongs can make….what was it again?"

But the old man lost his train of thought, and started to talk about something else. Felix tuned him out and thought again about his brother. His happy, fulfilled, successful, married, handsome, well-off brother. Somehow his image of Robert didn't sync at all with the word the policeman had used, with that word "suicide," with the image of a brother diced up like an onion by his own will.

Felix held the picture to his breast, and began to listen to his father again, who had now begun a recital of the last pages of Anna Karenina— lost, as every other night, in the static volumes of his broken mind.

As Anna went under her train and something monstrous and inflexible struck her head, Felix leaned back and let the pills numb him.

But somehow he knew there would never be enough medicine in the world to numb this. It was a pain that would never, ever die.

At long last he cried, his eyes closed tight against the heat of the fire.

Chapter 4

It just so happened that, like so many born rich, the idea of money as a life trajectory seemed silly to Felix Herbert. He'd had the luxury to feel this way his whole brief existence.

The slaughter, packaging, and shipping of pork flesh was the source of the family's great wealth. Heir to a ham fortune, Felix was. The cartoon picture of Herberta the sow on plastic shrink wrap, lain over the salty meat of a pig, could be found in delis and grocery stores across the Gulf South.

But the smell of shit and the candor of factory farm hands, the endless negotiation with suppliers, distributors, farmers: it all did little for him. He disliked seeing the rotund creatures snorting at their grates and waiting to die, witnessing their nothing-lives. The purposelessness of them made him sick someplace deep in the gut.

It wasn't that Felix was some kind of champion to animals. It was just too close to home, in a variety of ways. The air of efficiency, the measurement, the crunching, churning of it all: he still ate the Herbert pork anyway, was shaped by the money it made. He had always kept a stiff upper lip and forgone complaining, hating to think of himself as spoiled and unappreciative.

But lately he could see that he *was* spoiled. Gone to seed before his time. He'd quietly decided that money and ease had ruined him, softened him like porcine chattel. After returning from abroad, he'd relinquished the running of the family business to a series of middle managers, the books to a team of trusted accountants, who all assured him the family fortunes were secure for the time being. Then he'd rented an apartment, gotten a job (on his own this time), and was trying his hardest to be just a regular Joe for a while.

And now here he was. When his mother finally returned from the coroner that night, around one, she went straight to bed without speaking to Felix.

So Felix decided to return to his small place by the river and grieve alone in austerity. That is where Tomás dropped him off— back at the squalid block of apartments that were eight hundred dollars a month for a single bedroom, eating up most of his humble paycheck.

It was clearly not a happy chore for the old man.

"Master Felix," Tomás said, eying his charge in the rearview mirror. "Why don't you reconsider? Let me set you up in the guest house. You always liked it out there. We can play games of pool. I'll make you a hot toddy. I can give you more Spanish lessons in the morning if you like. We will talk if you want to, or not if you don't want to. I'll keep your Mother away too, if that is what you want."

Felix had begun sobbing in the backseat. When the dome light came on, exposing him, it became too much to bear. He managed to say, "No thanks. I'll see you soon Tomás," before crawling out of the car in front of his security gate and cursing himself a coward.

He stuck his head in the window of the idling car. "Do me a favor Tomás."

"Anything."

"Drop the 'master' shtick. You're my best friend."

Tomás looked at the steering wheel and then back to Felix. He nodded with a sad smile.

Inside and alone, Felix sat cross-legged against a wall and let the sobbing burn itself out. He had still not unpacked anything except for one box of jigsaw puzzles Tomás had gifted him.

To distract himself, he turned on his cell phone for the first time in days, and while it buzzed to life, he tried to hone in on the incomplete puzzle he'd been fooling around with in between shifts. The Sistine chapel – or a portion of it anyway – sad and broken, with all its half-formed angels and a man reaching for The Divinity that hadn't yet been put into place.

Coming back from the empty refrigerator, he listened to his reborn phone's many pings and buzzes. The green message light blinked out into the dimness of the apartment.

The first message was from sort of an ex, pseudo-girlfriend. She was angry, as she often seemed to be with Felix. He deleted the message before it concluded, blowing air out of his mouth.

The second message was from his dead brother, dated at 9 AM that morning.

"Hey Felix, this is Robert…I see your phone is going straight to voicemail again. Plug the damn thing in man. How's it going at your restaurant? I'm proud of you for getting that job, real proud. Angelica and I have been meaning to come eat for a while now, but I've just been so busy with…stuff. But you know, Carnival is on the way. And listen, I managed to pull some strings and I got you a spot to ride in the 13th float from the back in Bacchus! I know, I know I'm not even in that Krewe, but the parade is going to be amazing. Kickass right? Anyway, I need to get your answer by next week. But obviously you are going to say yes right? You can't turn that down bro… and the party afterwards, well, we all know how you like to party Felix. Say no more right? I'm just kidding around. I know you are probably feeling weird about the whole thing in Europe, but it really doesn't matter in the grand scheme of things, you know? No hard feelings. I would have spent that money on some bullshit Carnival dues anyway. I'm glad it helped you have a cool experience. I know you're just young and will figure it out sooner or later. Don't worry about what Mom says. She's got her own set of troubles she should be worried about, you know?"

A pause: kids yelling in the background, his wife's voice.

34

"Well, it's been a while since I've talked to you, so charge that phone up and give me a call soon. Miss you brother. I love you."

And then there was one message from his mother and three from Tomás. He knew what they were about and so he spared himself from having to relive it all again.

An hour passed, and then another, and still he sat listening to Robert's message again and again. The sobbing was over. There was a different part of him that was listening now. A part separate from grief and sadness and inevitability.

Instead: anger, bitterness, raw disbelief.

It wasn't the kind of message that a person left the morning before they planned on killing themselves. It was just Robert, normal as ever, happy, a little judgmental in that big-brotherly way, that warmly expectant insistence. Unless something awful had taken place in the 12 or so hours between the message and his death, Robert had not committed suicide. Felix knew it then. It was unequivocal down in his guts. But this did nothing but launch a thousand other questions.

If not suicide, then what was it, or who was it, that caused him to be under that train?

Who could he bring this raw feeling to? And what if he were wrong? What if it dug up some horrible infidelity in Robert's marriage, some terrible secret that would besmirch his name? What kind of skeletons might there be?

He couldn't go to his mother, couldn't stand up straight in front of her chilly power and pronounce that a voice message had convinced him that her best son's death had been an accident or even, something more. Would the police want to hear a message like this? Maybe. Maybe they would?

It would be impossible to sleep now— the pills, the heavy open-endedness, the trauma. He knew he ought to remain at home with his jigsaws, to piece together the cherubs and have a sensible cup of tea (a phrase his brother had always foisted upon his mother in between her cocktails) and try, try desperately to surrender to a decent, fortifying night of sleep.

But Felix wasn't sensible, even in far better moments than this one. And before he knew it he rocked on the streetcar rolling down towards the Quarter, where he knew he would linger until the calliope organ sent him stumbling back towards home in the foggy morning.

It was 3 AM by the time he arrived in the quiet pub on Esplanade, right where the tourist agenda of the Quarter faded into the more residential blocks of the outer Faubourg. The streets there were mostly empty on a weeknight, and the rows of townhouses sat solemn and spiky in the dim night. A winter air tasting of vomit and algae blew through the oak leaves.

They knew him there. He had a habit of spending nights in this particular pub when he felt restless, chatting to strangers and watching fistfights, sometimes napping on the bar. It was another step towards the average Joe he hoped to become, a place to feel like a normal person, and he had trouble sleeping in his new apartment anyway. The bartenders and regulars knew him there but it had never seemed to Felix to be a warm knowing. He wondered if this was just the way of such places or if there was something about him that put people on their guard, some aura of inhumane efficiency that had rubbed off on him from the pig factories. Or perhaps it was just the unearned levity that sons of the rich take on. Whatever it was, those sailors and longshoremen, roughnecks and truck drivers who seemed to never sleep— it felt as though they recognized not only his face, but also the myriad ways in which he was separate from themselves. They fought in their own circles, roared with laughter at each other, but with Felix kept the conversation light and distantly polite. They left him outside of the campfire, like some foreign visitor, but they never troubled him either. It was just as he liked it. He was both alone and not alone. Enough so to think clearly but to keep the darkest thoughts at bay, growling just beyond the neon lights.

He didn't even want a drink now, but he ordered a gin and tonic anyway so that it would sit in front of him and make him look more normal, and so that they would let him sit in there. A group of Japanese sailors sat at a table in the corner arm-wrestling loudly, while Felix watched the condensation form on his glass, replaying the voice-mail again and again in his mind.

"I know you are probably feeling weird about the whole thing in Europe," Felix whispered just above the roiling of the tonic water's bubbles.

That whole thing in Europe.

Three months. That's how long it had taken him to burn through the money his brother had "loaned" him to last a year. And what did he have to show for it? A few stories that every other young guy with a backpack and free time picks up. He'd failed at what he set out to do, and his brother was gracious enough to not ask too many questions, but brotherly enough to mention it the last few times they spoke, even if it was in the comforting language of condolence and forgiveness.

Felix just didn't care about teaching English. He thought he might have. He wished he could have. But in the end he didn't study. It felt pointless and without purpose. So he played, and when even the playing stopped being interesting he'd sort of just wandered off, taking a bus to Vienna where he tried to engage in the museums and grand buildings before feeling a wave of depression and melancholy crash over him, at which point he booked a ticket home with the last of the money.

At least he had the character to feel ashamed of himself, he thought. But it didn't help.

Sipping the gin, he thought through this and a lot of other things. Finally, he thought of the future, about the new world that would have to be lived in now without Robert. His sort-of nephews, his sister-in-law, the medical practice— all of these images appeared. Which one to worry about first? After an hour passed, Felix drooped down onto the bar and fell asleep.

It was right at daylight that the bartender, who wore a dress but had the cheekbones of an old man, nudged him awake and asked him to pay.

"Morning honey. You been asleep a few hours. Nobody messed with you though, I made sure. Go on now and pay your tab. The morning boy is coming in now and I gots to go home and sleep too."

Felix yawned, put a five on the bar and asked her or him to turn on the news.

And there it was, the first story after a long commercial for some new drug. The side effects were listed in a quick, peppy voice over a family playing in an English tea garden. Then the newsflash.

"And a shocking story from last night as a man was struck and killed by a train bound for the Greater Mississippi Wharf. Police say that Robert Herbert, a medical doctor and a prominent local citizen was on the tracks at the time that the eight o'clock train passed near the levy behind the Audubon Zoo. We are told at this time that the authorities are still exploring all possibilities, but will likely rule the death as a suicide. Lucy Williams, our veteran reporter, was able to get exclusive access to train conductor James LeBlanc, the sole witness of the accident and the person operating the train at the time. Having been cleared of all charges, Mr. LeBlanc had this to say to Mrs. Williams."

A man came on the screen then. Behind him was the police station, buzzing even in the darkness of the night. The man looked haggard, scared, like maybe the reporter had been chasing him for a bit through the parking lot and he had finally stopped and surrendered to his fate. He peered at the camera through sick eyes.

"Can you tell us what happened?" a woman's voice said. James LeBlanc flinched as a microphone was shoved into his face.

"A man was killed. He was in front of the train. I couldn't stop in time."

"Can you tell us anything else? Did you see anything suspicious? Anything?"

The man's eyes went wide then and he said, "I can't do this. I've gotta get home. It's been a long day, sister."

There was definitely something hiding in the man's performance, something behind his wide-eyed fear. Felix knew it as sure as he'd ever known anything.

There were some American soldiers at the end of the bar now. At least they wore American soldier uniforms. They were laughing and talking and Felix caught the phrase "rich person problems" come out of one of them.

It gave him an idea. Felix checked his watch.

He called his Mother, "Mom, is the offer for the money still on the table? It's not for me, it's for Robert. I've got something I have to do."

Chapter 5

His mother met him at the door the next evening. Since Felix could remember, it had always been Tomás who answered the doorbell. But this time she met him there on the grand porch, and with a check for five thousand dollars in her outstretched hand. His mother still used checks, wore dresses while alone in her own home, confirmed appointments with a phone call rather than a text message. In the "For" blank of the check she had written "My Son."

Her face was drawn taut and her eyes were red, tired. Felix took her in. He was as tall as her, shared her pronounced chin and long, feminine eyelashes. As he slipped the check into his front pocket, he produced a weak smile and a whole host of things he might say to his mother spilled into his mind: promises, memories, reassurances, and, of course, so many questions. What had she seen at the coroner's office? Would she be able to describe it in that tasteful, restrained way of hers? Had it shocked her to the point of silence, or had she cried out and crumpled? How horrible it must have been.

To break the silence, he asked some trivial question about the funeral arrangements and got a long and comprehensive answer, full of practical detail. And thus, they avoided having to talk about Robert.

He walked to the bank to cash the check. Felix was afraid his plan for this money was a bad one. With the cash in hand, his anxiety grew even worse. All sorts of headlines came to him as he made the long walk down to the Alabo Street wharf.

"Disgraced Scion Breaks Security Laws Set Forth in Patriot Act, Sent to Guantanamo."

"Grieving Brother Shot at Port Checkpoint."

"Witnesses Say Trespassing Heir Disheveled, Incoherent. Dragged Off by Longshoremen."

But while his confidence was flagging, reality turned out to be far simpler than he might have imagined. He encountered only one security checkpoint. A man sat hunched over in a booth, lazily poking at his cell phone. He was fat, and his slow eyes rolled across Felix without concern or surprise. The man's mustache was clearly the most animated thing about him, but when the phrase "two hundred dollars" was mentioned, the guard suddenly came alive. To Felix's intense surprise, not a single question was put to him about *why* he might want to sneak into a wharf. Afterwards the man avoided Felix with his eyes. It was a bit frightening how easy it was to slip in. It wasn't like he'd expected. Perhaps they kept the real security for the airport, Felix thought.

In such a way Felix found himself leaned up against a blue warehouse and waiting for the eight o'clock train to roll into the wharf. He spent a while admiring the place.

The river turned golden. Robert would never see it again, but that Mississippi sunset was still alive and well. There was still that.

Then the light was gone and the port blinked with hundreds of fluorescent lampposts. Arms lowered, bells clanged, and sad horns wailed. The eight o'clock train came grinding in. A crane began to lift the heavy, red boxes off its back and swing them onto a waiting barge. Felix watched a tired man climb from the conductor's cabin— the man from the news report, and he looked even more harried now than he had trying to escape the reporter in front of the police station. Felix's hunch had been right. The man hadn't even taken a single day off after the incident. Robert was dead, yet the world just went right along with its nose to the grindstone, seeing that the trains ran on time. He hoped the man wouldn't take one look at him and spit.

James the conductor punched a code into the door of one of the warehouses, and Felix timed it so that he was lunging from around the corner of that warehouse at precisely the correct moment, sticking his foot in the jamb just before it swung closed.

"Hello Mr. LeBlanc," Felix said, calling out to the man's back through the crack in the door.

James turned, slumping down when he saw Felix. He peered past the young man, looking for a camera crew maybe.

"My name is James."

Felix tried to smile. "It's just me, James."

But the conductor was still shaking his head and waving his hands. "I'm not supposed to talk to journalists, and even if I could, I don't want to."

"I'm not a journalist James, I'm Robert Herbert's little brother."

Now James squinted. "Christ."

There were deep lines around his eyes. He hadn't shaved and unruly hair poked out the back of his mesh trucker's cap. A deep sigh rolled out of the man.

"Look, I'm not here to make you feel bad. No one blames you. I really just want to talk to you about what happened," Felix tried, taking a slow step closer.

LeBlanc didn't say anything. He turned his back on Felix and walked into his office— but he left the door open.

There were no windows or plants in the small room. A picture of a German shepherd, a bowling trophy, a rack of hats. The roll of hundreds bulged in Felix's front pocket.

James rubbed his closed eyes and spoke to him. "Is there something I can do for you? I mean, is there anyway…some way I can make this easier? What do you want me to say? I'll say it, I just, I'm not sure I should say anything. I'm sure I'll just make it all worse. You know how trains work right? I mean, you know they can't stop that quickly."

The conductor put his face in his hands. His voice had cracked on the word *"stop."* Felix waited to see if the man would go on, but he didn't.

"James?"

The conductor had started to heave. "What do you want?"

"I just want to know what happened. I don't think it is an unfair request. See, I made a mistake. I came here with a wad of cash, James, ready to pay for anything I could get. But I can see you now. It isn't about money to you, right? I can see that money would be an insult here. But I'll just level with you James. There is no reason to think my brother committed suicide. I mean, I'm sure that is what people always say when a loved one offs themselves. They probably say, 'I'm sure there is more to it', and 'he would never do something like that.' So here I am. I'm still at the point where I don't know if I'm going crazy, falling through all those stages of grief that people always talk about. Maybe I'm just out of my head. But when I saw you on the TV something just felt wrong. Like I could see you were a good man who was hurting, and part of the reason you were hurting was that there was something you needed to get out but just couldn't for whatever reason."

James blew his nose, pointed a quivering chin up towards Felix. There was most certainly something there, a weight too ponderous to bear.

Felix leaned forward. "James. If you just tell me that there is nothing else to it and that I'm just…well, temporarily crazy with grief, maybe I'll just drop this thing here and now. I'll bury my brother. Tell his step-kids that their daddy was just ill. That everything they knew about him was wrong. That he kept some secret darkness in his heart while he was pushing them on the swing. But I don't think that is what you want me telling those kids James. Because if there is something else, anything else. I have to know about it. I have to know *now*. I have to know about it so I can know I'm not crazy and that there is something I need to figure out. Whatever it is James, I promise to leave you out of it. I'll just ask you to help my family by telling me the truth. Because I know a good man like you wants that opportunity. And I don't think you can go on without getting it off your chest."

Felix had said too much, too quickly. He tried to set his teeth against the further flood of words trying to spill out of his mouth.

LeBlanc blinked, pulling a finger across his eyes. "It wasn't my fault… I couldn't afford to lose this job."

"Why would you lose your job James?"

The conductor turned his palms upward.

"There was this cop."

"You mean there was a cop with him when he died?"

"No. In the station. When they brought me in. He turned off the camera and the microphone. He said all I had to do was forget." James' hands balled up into fists, and he slid them back and forth across his desk.

"He told me they had found barbiturates in my urine. Cocaine. Pills. He used the word manslaughter. He brought in this lady doctor who confirmed the test. I told her I hadn't been into drugs since the nineties and she told me it didn't matter. Then she left. The cop came back and told me all that mattered was that I forget about the mask. The mask with the angel corkscrew."

"What?"

There was a long pause. James was wavering.

"Your brother. He was….wearing a mask. He was kneeling, away from me, but at first, I thought he was looking right at me, because he was wearing a mask on the back of his head. A mask with an angel corkscrew on it."

Voices could be heard out in the warehouse. A laugh echoed down the tin siding.

"What are you talking about?"

James reddened. "He was wearing some kind of a carnival mask ok? He was wearing it backwards on his head. So it looked like he was facing me. That's all I can tell you. I've no fucking clue why everyone cares about it so much."

"But he had….you said he had an angel corkscrew?"

LeBlanc let out a breath. His eyes squinted up towards the fluorescent bulbs and the color went out of them.

"It was like he was wearing some sort of a costume. I saw it for just a second. But it looked like one of those corkscrews."

"Like…for opening a wine bottle?"

"Yeah, I guess. Maybe."

"And then what?"

"He disappeared under the train."

"But you never said anything about this in the official statement?"

"No. The cop went away, and then, later, this old detective guy came in. And I…I didn't say anything about it to him. Melan…Melancon. I just kept thinking about that lady doctor, about the paper she showed me. It said a thing about cocaine and barbiturates. Then she made us pray together. Told me to forget about what I'd seen and when I nodded my head she told me she'd keep the drug test in the bottom of her deepest drawer. But, I didn't tell. Are you going to go to the authorities? Are you going to tell?"

"You don't have to worry about anything," Felix said, but he wasn't so sure if that was the truth.

LeBlanc had put his head down on his desk. He was suffering, that much was clear. Felix counted out two thousand dollars and laid it next to him.

"This is for your shrink, if you find you need one. Or a bottle, or whatever it is to help you get through this. Just remember that you did the right thing here."

The conductor looked at the bills on the desk and shook his head.

"Just tell me who he was," James demanded.

"He was my brother. A doctor. A great man. He was a family man and he liked Mardi Gras quite a bit...Have a drink at Carnival for him, would ya?"

The conductor leaned back at his desk, wiped the tears from his eyes, and said, "I'm sorry."

Felix stood and put a hand on James' shoulder. "For what it's worth, you are forgiven James. A hundred percent."

Chapter 6

It was a nearly three-mile hike from the wharf to the site of Robert's death, but Felix needed time for some thinking. A walk might help with that, and though he couldn't have said why, the scene of the crime felt like the next place he ought to go, like the logical progression. It was dark and he had to mind himself a bit now, but he felt drawn by a strange energy.

He walked and thought. The initial pain of loss was already beginning to fade in its sharpness, replaced now by a dull thud at his heart, an ache that he knew would live there for years to come, always poking at him when he called Robert to mind.

The angel corkscrew, the cop, the strange doctor woman, the drug test. As he turned the story over in his head he couldn't quite see it, couldn't quite make it a reality. James seemed honest, solid, the type that couldn't and wouldn't come up with something so fantastic without it being truly so.

What did that mean? He thought hard about it, plodding over the broken sidewalks, but his mind drifted, leaden and cloudy. Sure, it was the stress, the trauma, the night spent face down on a bar counter. But there was something else clouding him as well, and he knew precisely what it was and what it was doing to him, could feel it deep in the pit of his soul. There was something gumming up the works. He'd been abusing his own mind for a while now, years of drifting along through things.

His legs grew tired around the second mile. He could see families eating dinner in their glowing kitchens. There was a weight to things, now. What happened next mattered. Life had consequences.

So, the decision settled on him over the course of three blocks.

"Local Boy Turns His Life Around."

"Young Man Shapes Up to Honor Slain(?) Brother."

"Sobriety And You: Ten Ways to Stop Being a Fuckup."

At the river, next to the Audubon zoo, he took a long sit, looking out at the lights of a weighted down freighter and knowing just what needed to be done. It was easy to know, but much heavier to do. The night wind came in cool and alive with Mississippi smells. Silt, rotting piers, long stalks of broken grass. He thought about all the things he could be. After a second, third, and fourth deliberation he summoned the courage to go through with it.

He scraped together a pile of gravel. Taking the pill bottle out of his backpack, he stared at it a moment. Those long, blue, lovely pills. Instant satisfaction. Sudden bouts of pressed happiness. Regret killer. Shame reducer. Joy Enhancer. He could coast on them if he wanted to. Could just take a few every time he thought about Robert until one day he'd forget about how to love.

Here were plenty of small, self-contained and instant spells of numbness, all leading down a gentle hill towards a soft end. He could even take it a step further. Speed up the process. He could ask his mom for a few grand and fly off to some place, some warm beach. Rent a bungalow by the shore and stick a needle in his arm until the world all faded away. He could fall into some nice brothel somewhere, give it all up and just have a cozy, warm, short life.

He remembered something Robert had said to him then, years ago when Felix had first been hit with teenage melancholy. What had they been talking about? He couldn't remember, only that he'd confided in his older brother that he often felt life had no meaning. That everything we said and did was meaningless in the end. And so what was the point of living at all? Typical teenage angst stuff.

Perhaps they had been drinking heavily that night. Robert had maybe not been so serious in what he said, but it stuck with Felix for the longest time, and bubbled to the surface now.

"You're still here aren't you," Robert had said, looking over his beer at him.

"Yeah, so what?" Felix had replied.

"Well, why aren't you dead yet, if life has no meaning?"

"I… well I suppose I could kill myself."

"But you won't," Robert had said, and looked at his little brother poignantly.

"I…"

"It doesn't matter what you say. The point is, you won't. And somewhere, deep in that little head of yours, is a reason why you won't. And that, right there, is your answer. The meaning of life is whatever reason you have for not killing yourself. And since you haven't done it yet, I suppose you already know your reasons."

The words took on such significance now, and looking at the little blue gems in their orange plastic bottle, Felix allowed himself to realize that he'd been avoiding the question for much too long now. He'd been avoiding everything. Time to choose. Live or die. None of this half-assed business.

He opened the top of the bottle and filled the empty space with rocks and gravel, sealed it back up again. Then he stood up and cast the bottle out as far as he could into the Mississippi. Thanks to the added weight of the rocks, it landed with a plop and disappeared, about twenty feet out into the current.

Robert deserved his whole mind, and Felix meant to give him that. Things were far from over.

He certainly did have a reason.

The angel corkscrew was the reason. It was a sealed, simple, message. But a message in a language Felix could not yet speak. That was the new meaning to his life. He decided it then and there in the darkness by the river.

Just a little further to go. He felt lighter, buoyant even as he walked along the bike path snaking alongside the levee. Until, at last, he came to it.

But it wasn't really grim. Not like he might have expected. The grass was still green and pale in the darkness, and the railroad tracks shone fresh and pure in the moonlight. The only signs of a death were the few strands of yellow police tape, now hanging loose and impotent from a row of lathes on side of the track. It seemed that commerce had resumed immediately without a hitch, and that set Felix to wondering about how many people had likely died on nearly every spot on earth, how every step he took was the sight of some trauma.

But it was time to settle his thoughts and focus. First, he made a wide loop around the place, circling in smaller and smaller from there. When he found a disturbance in the soil, mud on the grass, the butt of a cigarette, he'd stop and bend low to it. He wasn't sure what he was looking for, and perhaps he'd seen a bit too much television, but just being there in that solemn place gave him a sense that he was on the scent of something, that it was only a matter of time. It was as if masked, angel corkscrew sporting foot soldiers might be hiding around a bush somewhere, and Felix needed only to jostle that bush with a stick before the men would

54

come bolting out, and battle, in all its simple finality, could be joined.

Walking down to the place where the river met the levee, he found footprints. They might have been from a fisherman, a dog walker, riparian lovers, or a thousand other things— but they were there. The telltale sign of a bateau being dragged up onto the silt of the Mississippi River bank was also in this place among the cypress trees, and then, scraps of rope someone must have used to tie...something. Felix paused to picture his brother being pushed up this earthen wall under duress, the killer jabbing some angel corkscrew into his back. But when he thought about it soberly, he knew it was all meaningless. Possibly coincidental. There was all kind of junk down by the shore— bottles, condoms, hooks and wire—the accoutrement of dozens of petty offenses, of people coming and going. A piece of rope or a footprint was interesting, but didn't mean much to him, and certainly wasn't evidence.

But he found himself lingering a few moments longer. Being at the site was strange, almost nauseating. The smell of trash and muddy water reminded him of the smell of blood. Some sort of seabirds were squawking in the willow above him, and the distant train rolling down the tracks seemed wicked coming in the darkness. Felix felt dizzy and a bit faint. It was time he walked home.

He began his trudge with heavy feet and far more questions than he had set out with, but the hour had come where it was ill-advised to go on a distracted, moon-lit stroll. At all times, but particularly after the restaurants closed around ten o'clock, drive-by muggings were a part of life in New Orleans, affecting rich and poor, young and old. Dog walkers learned to beware. Chefs getting off the late shift came to carry their kitchen knives home with them. The thieves carried pistols. So, Felix just so happened to be paying more attention to the world than he usually did. It was because of this wariness that he first noticed the black Plymouth slowing behind him while it was still a block off.

As it came closer, details began to emerge. The car was distinctly unsexy. The tinted windows were rolled up and the brights were on, making it hard for Felix to tell what was going on in the cab. At 100 feet or so, the car seemed to notice Felix watching it over his shoulder, because it pulled over. It could have simply been a late-night bar patron returning home in that cautious, hesitant way that the more responsible drunk drivers tended to favor. But it was midnight now, and so Felix quickened his pace considerably.

But on the next block, it was there, and the next. At the corner of Laurel and Webster Felix stopped, stepping into the little corner pub there, which happened to still be buzzing. He sat at the bar with a Shirley Temple for a calculated ten minutes, but when he looked out of the front door the black Plymouth was still there.

He tried to picture what would happen if he just went up and knocked on the window. The people inside obviously knew that he was aware that he was being followed. Should he try calling the police? It would take them an hour to arrive, during which time the car could leave or else enact whatever nefarious purpose they had in mind. And when the cops did show up? They would be angry and unresponsive. They had murders to deal with, after all, and would probably dress Felix down quite a bit for having the audacity to phone them out over a parked car.

Felix wished he had a pistol, but he reasoned that if this car had come to visit some sort of violence on him they would have done it already. So, their purpose must be only to scare him, or to gather information.

With that in mind, he pulled out his cell phone, dialed Tomás, and walked out of the bar. As he walked, and the sedan followed, he explained everything to the old man.

"Someone is following me right now. They are in a black Plymouth. I'm headed down Coliseum Street. I'm going to take them to some apartments a few blocks from here and try to convince them that I live there."

Felix could already hear the old man throwing on his clothes – the jangling of keys and the scuff of loafers.

"You don't need to do anything Tomás. These guys aren't out to hurt me. Not yet anyway. I just wanted you to know. In case…about the angel corkscrew mask."

And as he was briskly walking, he related the events of the night to his old friend.

Felix quickly arrived at the nearby apartment complex and ducked into a stairwell, where he sat panting for ten minutes.

By the time Tomás showed up, there was still so much more to tell, but the black Plymouth had vanished back into the night.

Chapter 7

The next morning found Felix standing in the sun with soft grass underfoot. On the green lawn of the Metairie cemetery there were at least two hundred other unsmiling people. His suit was uncomfortable and he was sweating, withdrawing from his drugs, heart-broken. He did his best to keep his chin up. Robert would have been pleased at that much, at least.

Looking out over the vast city of the dead – the dust generals, the interred kings of Carnival, the masons and the captains of industry – Felix wondered if his mother would cry. She never cried. *Why does she never cry?* He thought about it through all eight verses of Amazing Grace, and felt that if *she* cried it would make it ok for him to cry. His father certainly wasn't going to be shedding any tears. The old man sat stump-like and uncomprehending in his wheelchair biting his lower lip until, half way through the hymn, he started reading the inscriptions on the stones aloud until Tomás tactfully wheeled him off a distance. Felix was jealous.

The family mausoleum had not been opened in some time, not since Felix's last grandparent died when he was sixteen.

But now it would open for Robert, or his ashes at least. It went against family custom to be cremated, but because of the nature of his death, there could be no open casket, no ritual goodbyes said over cold hands. Cremation was certainly best in this case.

Felix was thinking about eternity, watching as his brother's ashes were sent down to molder into the dust of his forbears.

"Ashes to ashes, dust to dust," the Father said. Then there was a long line of hand shakers who all said variations of the same thing. Most of them were doctors with cold hands. Many wore glasses and had strong grips, reassuring, medicinal smells. He didn't recognize most of them. Then it was on to Robert's home with the family.

The home was a creole style cottage just a few blocks off the Carrollton streetcar line. The rose bushes were the envy of the neighborhood, and the porch was wide and sunny with dual swing sets. Felix felt awkward. Robert usually came to see him wherever he was. He hadn't been invited over to this place often, and it was alien and unfamiliar to him, despite its loveliness and decorum.

Angelica, Robert's wife, was mostly silent, as were the two boys. The boys did not belong to Robert in the biological sense. They were squat and round, well-behaved and interested in card games and model building. But Robert had loved them, and taken on all the duties of a father with gusto. They'd called him Daddy.

They stood together in a little cluster by the hearth, weakly nodding at the people forming a circle around them. Felix hovered as near to them as he dared, tightly smiling over his plate of potato salad and waiting for them to say something, anything. The boys, George and David, stood there quivering and reserved. Felix had thought, on many occasions, that Angelica had probably told the boys not to get too close to him.

He went into the kitchen, where extended family members were ringed around the island looking sadly at their plates, drinking red wine, and whispering things about Robert. Felix shook hands with three male cousins, rubbed a new baby on the cheek, and kissed two other aunts before he was able to wend his way to the base of the stairs leading up to the attic office his brother had kept.

He crept up, feeling a wave of hot embarrassment flow into his cheeks. Why did he feel so criminal in his own brother's home? He should have every right, as the grieving little brother, to stand in his dead sibling's office, and perhaps even snoop around a bit, on the suspicion of foul play. He was going to need to stop being so hesitant, he decided. But the headlines still flashed before his eyes, as always.

"Bad Brother Busted."

"Loser Disrupts Solemn Wake."

"How to Ruin a Funeral in Ten Easy Steps."

And most importantly: "Can You Spot the Angel Corkscrew?"

Robert had been a neat, somewhat fastidious person, and his office had been left in an immaculate state. That was good, Felix thought. It would be easy and quick and perhaps he could find what he needed without causing a fuss.

But what was it he needed? He hadn't the faintest clue as he hovered around, moral hesitancy sliding its way up his spine. It wasn't as if finding an actual angel corkscrew would mean anything other than his brother liked a good pinot. So what then?

Perhaps the snooping ought to be of a more general nature, he decided.

What kind of plans would a suicidal person make, and how would they differ from a murder victim's? Would there be a receipt for a firearm somewhere in this stack of papers? An invoice for locks changed? Nothing like that. What would he have on his calendar?

The leather date book caught Felix's eye where it rested, the only item in the front drawer of Robert's desk. Somehow, taking something from a drawer felt a bit more nefarious than glancing at the papers up on the surface. Still, he found himself laying the book open on top of his brother's closed laptop.

There was nothing too interesting about the days leading up to Robert's death, at least not as indicated by this list of doctoral and domestic intimacies. David's soccer game. An advisory meeting with a group of residents. A reminder to make dinner reservations for Valentine's day.

"DEADLINE FOR CPA," one urgent scribble read.

"Call back Pharm Rep," on another line.

But turning the page and looking into the future, Felix saw a circle around the coming Saturday. Circled, in a red and more deliberate lettering, the note read "*Asclepius Ball.*"

"Asclepius," Felix said aloud, just before hearing the unmistakable sound of high heels coming up the stairs. He closed the book and walked over to a selection of photographs, posing himself there as if he were simply engrossed in memory.

Angelica's brow was already furrowed in annoyance, just as he might have guessed. She placed her arms akimbo, started to speak and stopped. It seemed she had purposely lowered the register of her voice.

"Felix," she said.

"Oh, hi Angelica, how you holding up?" He pretended to be surprised, casual.

She looked from the desk to the photographs and then back to Felix. "What's going on?"

"I was just…"

"Your mother needs you Felix." She moved aside, leaving a path open for him. "You should stay by her during this. She's alone you know."

"I…" Felix looked at her dry blue eyes, her slim face. She had taken off her black veil at some point and her makeup was so white and perfect that she looked like a porcelain doll.

Maybe he didn't understand. Maybe he did. Honesty swelled up in him for a moment and he felt the desire to share his burden with her. There was so much he could tell her, and maybe vice versa. Maybe he could begin by asking about this *Asclepius*. Or about the image of an angel corkscrew and how it might have been a part of Robert. As he thought these things the woman in front of him raised her jaw just a fraction of an inch. In that strange angle of her head, with those fortified button eyes and tired slouch of her shoulders, Felix suddenly saw her clearly. She was in a hurry. She was in a great rush to have all of this finished, folded away in a drawer somewhere. Probably to go out, hunt up another bread winner, and get the paperwork done and filed in the courthouse. It struck him that any questions, any continuation or open-endedness he suggested would be, in her mind, further proof that nothing good had ever come out of her husband's little brother. He ought to hug her if she would let him, say that he was sorry, and then ignore her entirely for years to come. At Christmas he should recall to her warm memories of his brother in a formal postcard. No more than that.

"I'm sorry," he said, and forwent the hug. As he walked down the stairs, he made a mental note to keep his distance from the family for the time being.

Downstairs Felix stood by his mother while people went past. The departing spoke to her, smiled at him and shook his hand. His mother received each of them with her polite acknowledgement, never wavering from her duty as the matriarch, never letting her hard smile falter. After a while,

Felix worked up the courage to put a hand on her shoulder. It was unclear whether she needed him to do so, but he wanted to anyway.

The stuffiness of the room, the condolences, the gin vapors, and then there it was— an angel corkscrew sitting alone on the kitchen island, trivial and mundane. He picked it up and carried it outside. He thought he might have picked a better week to start making life changes.

Out in the sunlight of the porch, he held the angel corkscrew out in front of him, studying it closely. What did it mean? Drinking? Drunk? Wine? Bacchus, the god of wine, had been the parade that Robert had somehow gotten him a spot in. What else could it mean? It was some kind of a key, after all. A key to... drunkenness? A key to good times? In vino veritas. Truth in wine. It was a long and twisting train of thought that ended when Tomás patted him on the back quite suddenly.

The old man looked grave and handsome in his tuxedo, perfectly ironed, and he straightened his white gloves before he extended one hand out to the young man.

"Felix." The two shook hands, but it felt to Felix like the warmest hug.

"Have you ever heard of something called Asclepius, Tomás?"

Tomás breathed in through his nose and he looked out into the yard, his head turned from the blooming roses that

Angelica took so much pride it, to the sad soccer ball, stuck in the corner of the fence.

But before Tomás could answer, Felix's father began to speak from the far corner of the porch, where he had somehow gotten his wheelchair between the railing and the swing and was peering at them from between the chains. Felix hadn't noticed him before now— his father had a way of doing that, of wheeling himself into some corner so that you nearly forgot about him until his next big oration.

"Apollo was never as famous a philanderer as Zeus himself, but he was also a God, for God's sake. He had his share of bastards to be sure. Couldn't keep it in his toga any better than the rest of them. And when you have a child by a God he comes out with GREAT WINGS, or goat feet maybe and…"

But Felix wasn't listening anymore, he had already pulled out his phone and begun Googling "Asclepius."

"Yup," he said. "Son of Apollo. Asclepius was often considered the God of Medicine."

"You are now becoming religious?" Tomás asked.

"Yeah." Felix looked over his shoulder, and then went on in a low voice. "Something like that. Robert had it in his notebook. He was going this Saturday. To a ball. Tomorrow. He had plans tomorrow. What does that tell you?"

"Well… I don't think I would make plans if I had decided to die. Or if I felt like my life was in grave danger somehow.

But...I'm sure I don't know anything about that, sir. Why would Robert go to a ball dedicated to a Roman God?"

"Sounds like a pretty normal Mardi Gras thing to me," Felix said, and he bent down to the old man in the wheelchair. "Thanks for the help Pop."

"KILLED BY A THUNDERBOLT. SMITTEN DOWN IN THE PRIME OF LIFE!"

"That's right Pop. We're all going to miss him. Now and for the rest of our lives."

Felix rubbed his eyes and stood up, thinking of what to do next.

"Would you like a ride, Felix?" Tomás asked.

"No, man, I think I'll walk, I've got to make some sort of plan."

He was halfway down the porch steps when Tomás called out to him.

"My boy...I..."

Felix cocked his head at Tomás, who stepped down onto the grass and leaned into him with an air of secrecy.

"You know...if you think this event might have something to do with Robert...I could ....perhaps ask around about this ball. I can't imagine that there would be any ball in the city without attendants of some sort."

"So you're saying you are part of the butler grapevine, Tomás?"

The old man straightened his back a bit. "Although it goes against the professional code of conduct, of course, circumstances being what they are I think...I would be willing to see what I can find, at least."

Felix smiled. "You're all I've got now Tomás."

The old man adjusted his tie, gave a hesitant nod, and looked back towards the porch, peering over the rosebushes.

Chapter 8

Felix was nearly halfway through the walk back to his apartment, and the day had grown warmer and more lovely. Maybe there was something about death that enhanced the world, beautified it, a subtraction that made the remainder more precious. He noticed all the little details— the way the oaks cracked in the wind, the blueness of the sky, and the way he felt as well. Restlessness in his limbs, some flu-like symptoms, and a sluggishness that was understandable considering recent events. But he had said goodbye to Robert, had accepted it. And now, here he was, above ground still, on this particular day in February, and in this particular green and old place. The pain would be there forever, he was certain of that, but it was just another part of his life now— a sad memory, a healed over wound, and from here he could grit his teeth and let go.

He would survive. In time, he might feel fine again.

At least, until he noticed the black Plymouth purring in his wake, creeping up, stalking him like a metal shark. It was the purr - that sound it made - that gave it away. The deep thrumming of the engine was like a predator growling in the bushes.

Felix wondered why whoever it was hiding in that metal shark hadn't chosen a quieter car. But maybe that was part of it. A feature not a bug. They must *intend* for him to see, to notice, and to be afraid. If that was the case, maybe they only had it in mind to scare him, and thus weren't as dangerous as he thought. But there was the Plymouth, trailing him with a slow roll, and immediately removing all the forward feelings that had been swirling through him on his long walk.

There was no doubt. He knew right away that it was the same car as before. Old and boxy and in the daylight now, it was much clearer just how much tint had gone into the windows. He couldn't see the slightest detail inside the cab. No movement or humanity of any kind penetrated the shroud. For a moment he stopped on the sidewalk while it crept along, watched it pulling to the curb once it got about fifty feet away.

Felix made a snap judgement— he wouldn't wait for things to develop this time. He'd just get clean away. It should be easy on foot.

And before giving it much more careful consideration than that, Felix took off. He ran, full sprint from the very start.

In his formal clothes, Felix bolted over the root-broken sidewalks off of Carrollton and let his expensive tie flop over his shoulder. The streetcar clanged from down the corridors of oak trees as he flashed past them. At Adams Street, he abandoned his clunky penny loafers, kicking them off at a trot so that he could pick up speed. The Plymouth stayed behind, ratcheted up now to a hum, honking its horn at a couple with a stroller crossing the street.

At the next block the Plymouth ran up alongside him, and he cast his eyes over his shoulder to glare at it. But still, he could see only his reflection in the inky black windows. As his lungs burned and his calves ached, Felix tried to weigh his own fear.

"Acting brave is being brave," he reminded himself between panicked breaths.

How easy it should be to lose a car in a residential neighborhood. But the opportunity hadn't yet come up— that chance to dart away from the beaten path of the sidewalk. Because that was really all there was to it, he thought to himself. All he had to do was find a path where they couldn't follow him.

Looking a block ahead, his escape route suddenly became clear. He knew where he was. It was just the spot: an old but rather expansive graveyard down the way, just a hundred yards or so.

He hooked a hard and sudden left turn that gave him a few seconds on the Plymouth, which was forced to come to a rolling halt at a stop sign. Both legs burned as he rounded the corner and saw the place where he would lose them. But the fence was at least six feet and the gate was locked. He

71

considered kicking it, but one look at the padlock was enough to relieve him of that notion. So he examined the fence again, topped with sharp looking spikes of wrought-iron.

The Plymouth was nearly on him now. Felix tore off his expensive coat and cast it up over the fence spikes of Carrolton Cemetery number one. Stepping back, he cupped his hands around two of the padded points and launched his body up and over the top. The spikes raked against his abdomen, pressing against his stomach and organs, but they did not pierce the coat. Landing hard, Felix rolled between two mausoleums, coming to rest on his back in the moldy earth. If they wanted to fight him they would have to do it on foot. He sat up and took the first thing to hand— an empty forty-ounce bottle. He smashed the bottom half of it on a stone corner, breaking it into a ring of daggers, and then went about losing himself among the raised graves. He was afraid now, and the setting wasn't helping. It was graveyards all day today, death hovering everywhere despite the sunshine and warm beauty of the afternoon.

"How to Survive a Foot Chase in 1000 Quick Steps."

He crouched and gripped his glass shard tightly. After a while his legs began to cramp. After an even longer while he decided to make his move, to make a getaway. He started a hunched over run, tripped on stones a few times, and came out to the corner of Lowerline and Hickory, peering between the bars for the black Plymouth. Not finding it, the thought crossed his mind that if they planned on shooting him, he would be better off flinging himself over some picket fence into someone's back yard as a next step. Make them shoot him in front of a wife sipping chardonnay and kids in a sandbox. Make it as public as possible. Don't let them hide it from the world like what had happened to Robert.

But the Plymouth was gone. He set down his glass bottle, he wouldn't be able to hold on to it while going over the fence without risking cutting himself. Felix climbed, slowly and carefully this time, and afterwards stood on the corner, catching his breath. He was filthy now with cemetery grime. His white shirt was ripped and he was shoeless.

When he saw the police car headed towards him down Lowerline, Felix bent over and breathed deeply, but only for the briefest of moments. In this pause, he had time to plan it all out— how he would straighten his tie, point backwards down the street, and explain in a breathless voice that someone villainous had been chasing him in a black Plymouth. He racked his mind for the plate numbers. Why had they been chasing him? The officers would want to know. And what would Felix say? *Well officer, it's because, obviously, there were men in the Plymouth worried that I, Felix Herbert, might find out about the angel corkscrew!*

"Psych Evaluations and You: How to Get Your Free Assessment."

But Felix had time, before the two officers climbed out of their cruiser, to have other, more sinister thoughts. To recall what the train conductor had said. If the wrong policeman could find Felix alone in a room with no cameras or recorders, what then?

His last thought, after that, was to continue running. But it was almost as if the police knew the signs of someone about to bolt, because as the idea was passing through Felix's mind they called out to him in commanding voices.

"Hands up," they yelled at Felix. It was a tone that didn't leave much space for conversation, for explaining, or for any expectation of help.

So he decided to say nothing, and reached for the oak canopy.

Both cops were white, which was a bit unusual for NOPD officers. Almost always a pair of cops would be mixed, one white and the other black. In fact, didn't he remember Robert saying that this was a policy of the department— to keep mixed partnerships in order to stave off accusations of institutional racism or officer bias?

One was older and had a cloud of curly hair circling a bald crown. The other was thin with hard puckered-out lips that suggested to Felix a lifetime of drinking whiskey straight.

The older man circled behind Felix. There was a shove. Now Felix found himself with his hands on the side of the police car, his legs being kicked apart. Officer Whiskey Lips, with his bony hands, began patting Felix all over.

"Where are the pills, son?" the older officer demanded.

"What?"

"We know you are in possession of controlled substances young man. Just tell us where they are and make it easy on yourself."

"No. What? I don't. I don't have any pills."

He almost felt the urge to apologize. A bony hand slid down the back of Felix's dress pants, feeling between his ass crack.

"He seems to be clean," Whiskey Lips finally admitted, giving Felix a chilly look. "Clean of drugs anyway."

"What?" The bald cop was surprised.

"Yeah, nothing."

The two officers stepped away from Felix for a minute, speaking together in a hushed tone. Felix heard the older officer say that his hands were tied.

"We could take him in for loitering maybe," Whiskey Lips said. This suggestion made officer baldy shake his head and throw up his hands.

"No, we let him go."

Whiskey Lips shrugged his shoulders and straightened his duty rig.

"Alright Felix," elder cop said. "Go home."

"Wait a minute. Just what the hell is going on here? You don't have a right to just show up and harass a citizen like this. And how do you know my name?"

Both men stood by the curb glaring at Felix until something told him to just shut up and walk away.

And so he did, and made it back home without further incident. Once back in his apartment he found himself checking the lock on his door every thirty minutes to make sure it was still bolted, and for the first time ever he used the additional chain to double safe it. Remembering something he'd seen in a film, he also went so far as to balance a spoon on his doorknob. A long wooden spoon went into the window jamb and made it harder to slide open.

But for all his cautions and preemptive measures, Felix found that he was still afraid, and wondered if this made him smart, or a coward. *Acting brave is being brave*, as Tomás was always fond of saying. He reminded himself that he'd done nothing disgraceful.

So far.

He slept a light, tussling sleep.

In the morning he reported into the kitchen for a day of work as he was scheduled to do.

Chapter 9

The kitchen grew quiet when Felix entered. The thrumming of knife blades slowed and a radio was turned down to mumble rap music in the background. The three hard hands looked at each other, and then at the young interloper. They walked toward him slowly, not meeting his eyes, each of them with a new patience. In turns they offered him fist bumps, pats on the back, and slow, knowing nods. Then they said nothing but stood around him lingering a moment, smiling in rough understanding. To Felix's shock Sweets leaned in and gave him a hug.

He tied his apron on and tried his best to make small talk, to ask about the specials, if they'd been busy, how far behind on prep work they were— which was not at all.

No one said the phrase "your brother" or the word "death." They avoided it gladly and took to the small talk with relish.

If Felix had been a bit stronger, he might have talked about it with them. Perhaps they might even offer some insight into the current predicament. Felix wondered, as he ran his knife along the greased whetstone, just how many details the kitchen hands might be aware of. Would they have any sense, any at all, of the looming uncertainty behind it all?

The shift started normally. An hour in, the scarce-seen executive chef materialized in the kitchen. He wasn't one to make chit chat or to stand around observing. On rare occasions, when he deigned to drink half as much and appear on the line, he was a whirlwind: a lanky force tallying veal cutlets, scooping penne, shuffling around with a clip board, and usually drinking red wine out of a large foam cup. The chef was lithe and ropy, asked many questions, and had a face weathered by artificial elements. He was the only person Felix had ever met that managed to slouch and yet seem at the same time to be vigorous and vital.

Finally the chef stopped his work and was quietly regarding Felix as the young man carefully battered a softshell crab for the fry pit.

"Where y'at Felix?"

Felix always felt this local phrase to be awkward to answer.

"I'm alright Chef."

The chef stood eerily still on the other side of the heat lamps, watching his movements. It made Felix nervous and he wasn't sure why.

"You keeping things clean over there?" the chef seemed to be looking down his nose at him, but smiling at the same time.

"Yes."

And as an afterthought, "Sir."

Felix had no idea where he stood with the chef. He tried focusing in on his work, losing himself in the rhythms of it, but the old man remained in his peripherals.

They were two hours into the lunch service when the health inspector arrived.

He was a little button-up man, as they tended to be, clean shaven with a boyish moon face. He stepped into the kitchen unannounced with his forms and his name tag and began taking notes on a yellow pad. It wasn't an unusual sight, but each time they stepped in, the kitchen would tense. It was an awful feeling to be covered in sweat and flour, and to have a clean man step in from his office to pass judgement on your labors. Felix knew what the workers on the pig-killing floor must have felt seeing him with a hardhat on, barely grown, being led around to surmise technique and speed.

"Sharks in the water," the grizzled chef said, quickly pouring the last of his wine into a sauce pan. He was fairly sauced himself, Felix reflected, but had one of those faces that you could barely tell.

"Good afternoon, gentlemen."

The man rocked on his heels while waiting for an answer, when none was given he turned his eyes around the kitchen.

"I notice there are no ladies back here with the pots and pans. I guess you keep them all up front where they can be appreciated," The man said, letting out a sensible chuckle. It was the sort of laugh that Felix recognized right away— that reserved, plastic laugh of the golf club.

No one else laughed, and the man's clipboard drooped to his side, crestfallen. He went about his work then. He bent under the salad station, remarked on the cleanliness of the floor. He ran his finger across the chrome of the prep table, peered up at the oven vents and crossed off his boxes.

Then he came to Felix's station, stopped, turned, looked at Felix with dark, shark-like eyes. It seemed abrupt, unnatural.

"Mind if I have a little look?"

The rhetoric of the question rubbed Felix the wrong way. The man hadn't looked inside any of the other cooking stations yet. But he had circled around and found his way here, to stop and ask that question with his glasses stuck in his shirt pocket.

"Be my guest," Felix said, crossing his arms and stepping away.

The man, still looking at Felix, wedged himself back onto the line. The mats were spotless, he remarked. Then he pulled open the metallic door of the refrigerated base of Felix's cooking station. The inspector moved around some eighth-pans of cheese, bacon, and fish filets, and then his arm went still.

"What's this?" the man said, and pulled out a bottle of roach poison that Felix had never seen before. The inspector tutted at the poison, his eyes darting furtive back to Felix.

"What the fucking, fuck Felix," the Chef was yelling, while the inspector just shook his head and tutted away, making dramatic clip board markings and arranging the offenses in a neat little row.

"Of course, you'll need to shut down until you are in compliance."

The chef seemed to wobble on his feet, lost in a haze, and then all at once snap to attention.

"Get out, you're fired," the chef said, pointing towards the door.

"Of course," Felix replied and dropped his apron on the ground. There was nothing else to do. He gathered his few pieces of accoutrement and walked out of the back door and into the potholed streets.

Just as he expected, the black Plymouth was there. He hadn't needed to go searching, to poke and prod back alleys or look behind any bushes. Just two blocks from the restaurant, parked a bit too close to the stop sign, with no indication that anyone was inside. Felix knew without giving it much thought at all.

As he approached the Plymouth, he watched for signs of life stirring within the blackness of the windows. Still nothing, as ever.

He pulled out his kitchen knife, and showed it to the dark windows. It was the one Robert had bought him as a congratulatory present on this new job, the one he was now carting home from being fired from that same job. Felix ran his fingers across the Japanese craftsmanship.

It took a bit of work before he weaseled the blade firmly into the side of the front left tire, right on the outside rim. Once it hung there, about an inch into the tire's flesh, he kicked it in the rest of the way.

The tire protested, whined, and flattened.

He had time to cut one more tire before a lady walking her poodle gave him cause to slip off down the street. The last thing he needed was those two cops showing up again.

When Felix arrived at his apartment complex, Tomás was waiting by the security gate. The old man looked worn in the face, but his coat and pants were as immaculately pressed as ever, and his loafers gleamed in dwindling daylight.

"Felix."

There were cats that lived there by the gate, and two of them sprinted out and ran to Tomás, who bent down and opened for them a tin of sardines.

"They got me fired from my job Tomás."

"*No.*"

"They put poison in my cooking station, set up a health inspector to find it. That's it for me. I won't be improving my knife skills until the next time around."

"But who are *they*, Felix?"

"Well, that's the question. I was hoping you could help me out with that," Felix said. "All I've got to work on right now is a black Plymouth and some Carnival ball."

"Yes… this Asclepius Ball, let's go inside and I'll fill you in."

Tomás began as they entered the apartment. "It appears to be associated with a minor Carnival Krewe, same name. The Krewe is on the books now, but only this year. First time ever. Apparently, it existed for some time but has only been properly ratified just now. As such, this is the first official ball, and it is looking to be extravagant. I'm told upwards of fifty grand is going towards the festivities. There is no secret here. Robert was definitely on the guest list."

Felix boiled water, "Why would it be a secret?"

Tomás looked up at the ceiling, silent.

"So, this is some kind of doctor thing?" Felix asked. "I mean…really it seems like this was just a physician's club that Robert was a part of. I don't think we need to follow up on this, do you? What would it have to do with…"

"Do you have a pen and paper sir?"

Felix placed a cup of tea in front of Tomás, who had yet to sit. "Let me see."

After some digging, the paper and pen were located. Tomás fixed his hands and began to draw. A few minutes later they were both staring down at a cryptic symbol drawn in child-like, squiggly strokes.

"Excuse me sir, damned arthritis."

"What are we looking at Tomás?"

Tomás walked into the kitchen and began digging around in the drawers. Finally he produced the object he'd been looking for, and laid it down on the table next to his drawing.

It was the angel corkscrew.

"Can you see a resemblance?"

He pointed to his drawing. "This is the symbol of the new Krewe."

"A corkscrew? Really?"

Tomás cleared his throat. "That, Felix, is a *caduceus*."

"A ca-what?"

"It's some kind of symbol for a doctor."

The two of them cocked their heads at the little sketch, and then looked at each other in grim understanding. Felix looked up the symbol on his phone.

There it was. A staff with a sharp, pointed end. Two snakes entwined around it in a corkscrew fashion. And at the top, grand angel wings. "I believe we have an opportunity to take one step closer to the truth," Tomás said, as he produced a scrap of paper from his coat pocket. "The address. Out in Spanish Turn. The Asclepius Ball. It is tomorrow night at the Troxclair mansion."

"Troxclair?"

"It is a great house, Felix. That is the first thing I know. It employs three manservants and a Czech au pair who is easily bribed with gifts of chocolate. The third thing I know is that the house is new, even for Spanish Turn standards."

Felix studied the address. "But do you know what the Troxclair's do? Doctors I guess?"

"I've heard vague reports that they work in the medical field sir, but I haven't had time to research them thoroughly. The name itself is fairly old, but not in any significant aspect. I believe they may be new to money."

"I see," Felix said.

They didn't talk for a while. The tea was forgotten and grew cold and bitter on the counter. Tomás stood looking out between the blinds and then, against Felix's protest, began dusting them with a rag.

"You still don't ever just sit down Tomás," Felix said.

"I've never got in the habit."

"Well save a bit of energy for the ball," the young man said with a smile. "We are going to need it, I believe."

Chapter 10

Spanish Turn was a bewildering sort of place. It was a monument to the flight of the wealthy, first. That migration of money out from city center that had begun decades ago was not so unusual, though. What did surprise the blue-collar guest, lawn man, cable technician, and construction crew was just how deep, just how far, and to what a swampy, low spot the wealthy would flee.

That you could have dry-cleaning delivered to a quag seemed outlandish. To have cables and asphalt running into a fetid marsh felt obscene. It gave the neighborhood a sense of mystery and decadence. An air of hubris.

What was it doing there? The saw palmettos and cypress knees didn't know. Alligator swamps surrounded three million dollar estates where termites moldered the baseboards. Algae laden tides lapped up into kidney shaped swimming pools, and miasma hovered over the 18th hole. It arrested one just what kind of succor money could really buy.

Felix admitted that the place had a bit of style – not a total over the top garishness – and he said as much to Tomás as they approached the checkpoint leading into the subdivision. Darkness had come, and the waving flashlight of the security guard reared up out of the night. Suddenly, a modern gatehouse flanked by brick and wrought iron appeared. A fat woman in a too-small uniform stood out in the street and peered at Tomás.

"Name and business"

"I present Master Don Demarest, on his way to visit the Troxclair estate."

She clicked her tablet a few times. "He's not on the list. Sorry, you'll have to back out. You're blocking the gate."

"Of course," Tomás said politely. "But I wonder if there might be some mistake."

"I can call up their security if you like."

"Ah, that won't be necessary." Tomás nodded, "A simple misunderstanding I'm sure. I'll phone them directly and try again once we've spoken."

He maneuvered the car around.

"Are we just going to give up that easily?" Felix asked. The guard shone her flashlight on their inspection sticker and then on their license plate as they pulled out.

"Of course not. But I couldn't well ram the barricade, Felix."

Tomás pulled down the highway a bit. Once the road had passed the turnoff to the subdivision, it grew even more desolate. Wide potholes began to appear, and the street lamps faded.

"You see, I was worried about this exact situation, so I prepared something," Tomás said, and he tossed Felix a backpack from the front passenger seat. Inside was a t-shirt and jeans, rubber boots, bug spray, and a headlamp.

"We go through the swamp, then?"

"Desperate times, Felix. If they've been trailing you, then they know who we are. Exactly who we are. Any security guard for miles has more than likely been told to be on the lookout for we two. The Demarests are friends of the house who happen to be wintering in Spain. It was a gamble to try the name, but I'm not without a backup plan."

"I'm glad you are on my side in this Tomás. I have to say, I didn't expect you to come around so…completely. You are already miles ahead of me. I hadn't even thought this far."

The old man was quiet for a second, and then said, "Imagine if you are right, and these people somehow…were involved in Robert's… I don't want to think about it, but the alternative…the idea that Master Robert, in the prime of his life and with a family to feed…was cut down…it's just, well…he was a bright and competent man your brother. Honorable and strong."

"You're right. He was," Felix said, and began changing out of his suit and tie for the swamp clothes. "These people *must* have something to do with this. I can feel it."

Tomás nodded and sighed in the front, unzipping his own backpack.

The first hurdle would be to find and climb a white, brick wall that had been built, at great expense no doubt considering its length, around the entirety of Spanish Turn. They would need to locate it in the darkness of the swamp and scale its slimy surface. Tomás laid out their path in great detail as they exited the vehicle.

"It shouldn't be far off of the highway," the older man said, flicking on his headlamp and crossing himself before he crossed the ditch. He had parked the car as far as he dared in some shrubs, but it was still visible from the highway to anyone looking. He couldn't risk getting it stuck, he said, and having no means of escape. It occurred to Felix just how much time his friend had been spending thinking about the details of this situation.

But the warm feeling for his elder confidant had no time to flower in Felix, as he found himself stumbling wildly into the first pool of stagnant water, noticing that smell of all things green and scaly and alive. He pulled his boots up out of the sucking mud and reminded himself what was at stake.

They were lucky enough to miss any chance encounters with fierce reptiles, and after a sweaty five-minute slog stumbled onto the moss covered white wall, looking downright archaeological rising up out of the algae pools. It might have been a Roman ruin from the look of it.

Felix went first supported by Tomás, who he then pulled up. For all its stature the wall seemed merely symbolic. Though

Tomás had to resort to the squeaky thrashing of his boot-heels for a few moments before finding purchase on the white paint, his scramble over was a minor struggle at most. On the other side, the partners found themselves kneeling on soft, tended grass, glistening in the back-porch light of a baroque style mansion.

Tomás pointed towards some hedges, which they ducked into and, as quickly as they could peel off the swampy, saturated clothing, changed back into their dinner jackets and slacks, stuffing the soiled jeans into the pack and leaving everything in the hedges. They then walked casually out into the street.

It was awkward walking along the main boulevard in such fine clothes. But of the expensive cars that passed them, not one seemed to give them a second glance.

After a ten minute walk Tomás pointed again.

"There sir. The Troxclair Estate."

There was no mistaking it as the place to be on this particular night— it was a beacon against the inky swamp, high on an artificial mound of clay that had no place in that bend in the river. It was one of those homes built new with the intent of looking old, and in particular it mimicked those cake-colored Victorian spreads that the Garden District so favored. Doric columns on the upper floor, a wraparound porch as white and angular as the guests milling up the sidewalks, and glowing purplish for the season. It could have been the house just next door from the Herbert manor back in the city.

"I plan to keep a low profile," Felix said, with a glance towards a group of wives in their sequined evening gowns. They seemed already loosened by alcohol, and laughed their rich laughs of leisure and abandon just a touch louder than Felix appreciated.

"I believe you will be 'made' as soon as you enter the foyer, Felix. But not to worry. We are protected by the public."

One of the boozy women slapped the other playfully on the shoulder and nearly lost her balance. Felix shuddered.

"The public, eh?"

They managed to get inside the great wooden doors, check their coats, and enter the main hall without incident. Out in the crowd, Felix tried to steady his breath, to look at ease, but he could feel a lump in his throat forming, a gagging sensation and a rising nausea. He found himself backing into a corner. The wall rose up behind him, and his palms went flat against it until he felt Tomás' hand gliding onto his shoulder and prying him out into the open again.

He gathered himself together and beamed a smile. It was time he scanned the faces in the room for hints of murderous capability. What did a killer look like? In real life? Were there signs and symptoms, rage in the angle of a jaw, a twitch to the eye maybe? He tried to imagine what a blood-stained hand might look like against the stem of a chardonnay glass, a killer's chest rising and falling beneath a cravat, a plainclothes villain discussing his golf score. But imagination quickly failed him, and he reminded himself that he knew nothing about these people. That this was all just a hunch based on a few loose bits of circumstantial evidence.

Felix leaned in towards Tomás. "Which one is Troxclair?"

"I'm not sure, but I believe we will shortly find out, one way or the other sir. Might I recommend a... *reconnaissance* mission of some kind?"

"Yeah. You might. If I can just loosen up a bit." Felix could feel the sweat pouring out of him.

"I may hate to admit it, but I'm a bit afraid Tomás. They might be murderers."

"Acting brave is being brave." Tomás smiled. "Now, your brother sir. Robert. It would be wise to stay focused."

Felix looked into the old man's eyes.

"You're right. We need to get upstairs, maybe, into his office. See what kind of stuff we find."

"I have great faith in you sir. And what should I do?"

"Wait down here. But watch who goes upstairs and if they look like they know where they are going... text me I guess."

"Good thinking Felix."

Felix wanted to shake the man's hand but caught himself. For some reason, the mission had taken on a sense of doom for him and he wanted to say some last words to Tomás. But he simply had to shake off his sentimentality for the moment.

The tinkling of a wine glass, and a hush fell over the crowd. A man stood up on a box of some sort, and addressed the crowd.

"Welcome, welcome, welcome, to the first *official* annual Krewe of Asclepius Ball. Stop me if you've heard this one before. A doctor and his wife were having a big argument at breakfast. 'You are terrible in the sack!' he shouts at her and storms off to the OR. By midmorning, he's calmed down a little bit and decided he'd better make amends, so he phones home. There is no answer, so he calls a few more times. Finally his wife picks up. 'What took you so long to answer?' the doctor asks. 'I was in bed,' the wife says. So he asks, 'What were you doing in bed this late?' 'Getting a second opinion,' she says."

So many rail-thin people, pretending to laugh, slapping backs, pearly teeth flashing in the night. The tinkle of ice cubes and the smell of cologne was everywhere. The man went on telling bad jokes, and making toasts to other doctors. As Felix gently maneuvered through the audience towards the staircase he arrived back at a sense of disdain. It was like passing among stalks of corn in a field. The earlier group of women, even boozier now, stood popping caviar crackers near the crystal punch bowl and the twenty year old bourbon, not listening to the speaker, who was now going on about all the charitable donations made to the group.

Felix began to climb the grand staircase. At the top he found himself in a long hallway with at least a dozen doors. Before he had much time to pick one, a door at the end of the hall swung open and a woman stepped out wearing a maid outfit. She smiled at Felix, and stopped in front of him.

"Can I help you sir?"

"Um..bathroom?"

She opened the door immediately on his left and waved her hand.

"The main bathroom for guests is downstairs in the pool house, for future reference?"

She sounded Australian maybe, the way her statement went up at the end like a question. But she was gone, on her way somewhere in a great hurry.

Felix stumbled into the bathroom. Potpourri smells and art deco.

Hanging on the wall opposite the mirror: a picture of a man and wife on some mountaintop, some sunrise, an anyplace view of purple hills in the distance. Beige and peach clothing, sunglasses. Felix snapped a picture of the photograph on his cell phone, but it wouldn't have mattered. That man's look was now implanted on his brain.

Curly hair. Feminine, almost bird-like features. A thin frame with long, patrician limbs and a chin-high, prideful bearing. This was a pretty man. But not tough. At least, Felix hoped not.

In his sizing up of the man, Felix neglected to pay much attention to the wife at his side in the picture.

Peeking out into the hall, Felix checked for any other staff before risking another door, and then another in the long corridor.

After two bedrooms and what looked like a home gym, he finally found a room that seemed to be an office.

There was nothing remarkable about the small room, classically decorated: that dusty bookishness a well-off doctor might favor.

And then he pulled open the desk drawer.

Felix, if it were not for his history as a great taker of pills, might not have recognized the long white pharmacy bottles. Nor would he have understood the names— the oxycodone, hydrocodone, fentanyl, meperidine and methadone.

There was one other bottle with a name he didn't recognize.

"Sco-po-dol," he read aloud.

He photographed the open drawer, and then opened another. He put his phone back in his jacket pocket and continued to look around.

On the desk, he noticed a plaque. King and Queen of Asclepius – 2017, Max and Lena Troxclair.

Felix felt the sickening vibration of his cell phone then, but it was too late to fish it out. And anyway, he could guess what it would say. As he slipped the drawers shut, the knob on the door to the study began to turn.

It swung open.

Chapter 11

Felix slammed himself down hard on the cypress floor behind the desk, knocking the wind out of his lungs. Not that such wind would have done him much good, with nowhere to run now anyway.

The door had opened, that was a fact. Here he was. He was caught. Felix felt sorry for himself in that strange moment.

"Two Brothers Buried Back to Back"

"Carnival Ball Turns Massacre"

"How to Make it Look Like an Accident in Five Easy Steps."

The light of the hallway poured in. Three incredible seconds passed where bravery and intelligence wrestled— but the silence stretched on, lingered. What followed in the silence was a brief optimism, the idea that it might just be that the person at the door was simply dropping off his coat and rejoining the party.

"The wicked spies on the righteous," a female voice said, smashing his hopes in an instant. The door closed quietly behind it.

There were few options now. He would have to stand, turn, and face the person behind that voice. Felix checked to see if his life was indeed flashing before his eyes. Nope. Just a dry feeling in the pit of his stomach and a ringing in his ears.

So he stood.

It was the woman from the picture, the wife of Max Troxclair, the woman that had only barely registered to him while he'd been looking at the photograph.

"Mrs. Troxclair?" he said, sizing her up in the dimness of the office.

"Lena," she said. "And you are Felix Herbert, no doubt."

Felix took her in as she flicked on a lamp. She had big, rosy lips, soft and high cheekbones, and a perfect nose. Her large blue eyes seemed to demand very little given the circumstances, were calm even. Then he noticed the rest of her.

Lena, Felix now came to gather as she stepped closer, had some sort of malformation. She had a hunchback. Yes, that is what he would have called it. A giant mound of flesh rising unpleasantly up from one shoulder. She walked with a limp, not at all graceful. One of her hands seemed shrunken.

But what a face to have attached to such a body. The face itself said *trophy wife*, but the body said *beast of burden*. It was an incongruous image, and Felix stood blinking at her in the dim light.

"I see you've stumbled into my office, do you like it?" Her shriveled hand waved in front of her, encompassing all. She had a twang to her voice, a candor in her misshapen gestures.

"It's just an office," he said, feeling flat and uncomfortable standing so close to her.

"Oh, you must have supposed that my *husband* was the occupant here. That he was the breadwinner of the family. A common mistake, I suppose. But have you seen my husband? I mean have you really looked at the man? Poor Max has never worked a day in his life I'm afraid. He is a professional playboy. But…who else do I know who was born into undeserved wealth…I wonder?"

Felix's lips went tight.

"He married well, anyway, my husband," she laughed. "A wife of noble character is her husband's crown, but a disgraceful wife is like decay in his bones."

"Um…" Felix began to mutter, growing red and charged in his corner. She stepped closer. He was trapped now by her tight, round form.

"But listen to me carrying on. Now what are we going to do about this, Felix….tsk, tsk, tsk."

He steeled himself as best as he was able, and took one clumsy step forward to meet her, knocking a globe off of its pedestal. They watched it bounce for a minute, and then Felix said: "I'm here because my brother is dead, because he was a member of this club, and I'm thinking maybe someone here knows something about it. He was wearing...he had a...mask on at the time of his death. A caduceus mask. Like a mask from *this* Krewe."

She snickered. Backing away from him, she walked to the opposing wall and began to pour herself a drink from a cart there.

"Yes, your brother," she said with her strange back to him. "He was a fine man. I was so sorry to hear about his suicide."

"That's the thing. Robert was happy. He was strong. He had kids and a wife and a practice and..."

"I've seen it before as a doctor Felix," she turned back to interrupt him, "sometimes people who appear whole on the outside are secretly nursing some dark pain. Just like you Felix. But we both know that isn't why you are really here."

"What do you mean, of course that's why I'm here."

Lena clucked her tongue and set down her drink on the desk, coming face to face with him, dangerously close now. He could smell the gin on her breath.

"A well-known junkie infiltrating the home of a prestigious doctor in the hopes of scoring a fix...tut tut....though I do suppose it makes for a good piece on the five o'clock news. Just imagine the headlines! Ah...but your poor mother has been through so much already, don't you suppose? A strong woman. I respect that. I think she can probably weather the blow. And you, her no good black sheep, can just sit in the pokey and think about what you've done."

At that moment there was a knock at the door.

"Entrez vous," she said. Two stout men entered the office and shut the door behind themselves.

Felix became angry, realizing the situation he was in. "I've seen the pills lady, seen your stash. There is no reason for you to have all these pills. All we've got to do is report you to the police and…"

Lena walked to her desk gracefully, pressed a small button.

"Judge not, lest ye be judged."

A voice came on the intercom, "Yes, Mrs. Troxclair?"

"We have a guest who is requesting a police presence, Scarlett."

"Yes ma'am, Earl and Smith?"

"Indeed."

Then she turned back to Felix. "I don't think you understand my boy. You've got a serious chemical cocktail in your system. You've come here, high on what amounts to an egregious amount of drugs, in an out of your mind attempt to score pills, and are simply creating some wild conspiracy to weasel your way out of it."

"But I'm stone sober."

"Are you?" She asked. "I doubt a blood test, or even a field sobriety test would confirm as much Felix. After all. Results can be…well let's just say that those tests are fickle."

Felix was close enough to her now to reach out and put his hands around her misshapen neck.

She seemed to read those thoughts. "And when we asked you to leave you turned violent. I believe you are familiar with Louisiana's 'stand your ground' laws, are you not?"

"You wouldn't."

But they would, and one of the men had already thrown him from behind the desk out into the middle of the room. As the first bear paw of a fist crashed into Felix's stomach, he hunched over, trying to protect his face. It was his first taste of real violence in a soft life, and he was surprised how little it hurt in the heat of the moment. He wasn't made of glass, it was surprising to learn. But then, the punches began to really sting, and he was saddened that he had brought Tomás into this, and sadder still that there really wasn't much he could do. One of the men reached into Felix's jacket pocket and removed his cell phone. By the fourth and fifth punch he was beginning to feel a blackness coming on.

When he came to, flashing blue and red lights were leaking in through the office window, and he was alone.

When the two officers arrived in the upstairs room, it took Felix a moment to put two and two together— he was dizzy from the beating. But the voices were unmistakable. He had met these two officers some place before. They had Tomás in cuffs already.

Felix struggled to get a solid look at the cop's faces as they pulled him out and down the stairs. He was sure of it— the same characters from before. It was the thin pickled lawman, the one Felix thought of as Whiskey Lips, and the cop of the bald crown and curly ring. The ones who had searched him for drugs just the day before.

Felix knew the futility of trying to sing his song about the drawers full of pills. He and Tomás were outnumbered, outmatched, outgunned.

"Make sure you lead them through the party, out the front door," he heard Lena saying to the officers from the landing of the stairs.

Felix and Tomás bore the humiliation bravely. They withstood the gasping looks, the sideways glances. You could have cut the smugness in that room with a knife. At the end the pair were summarily thrown into the back of the squad car. They were not questioned, read any rights.

Curly wasn't even out of the neighborhood before he started talking about alligators. "You know, Earl, when I was working homicide, the times we would find a body in the swamp, there would be almost nothing left. Very little to identify with. I mean, sometimes you could get a few teeth if you sorted through the gator shit, but usually not a complete set. That made the job pretty tough man, but hell, at least we had a union in them days."

Pucker-up Earl responded, and in the street lamps passing from different angles, Felix could see that the face which had appeared so deliberately scrunched was actually the result of a series of scars.

"That's only if the river don't get em'. When I used to work Harbor unit, we'd find a body a week in the river. I mean just think about it, that whole river goes basically from Colorado to Pennsylvania and all points in between. Can you imagine all the blood, fingers, toes, and whole bodies that end up in there? It's like a bunch of puzzle pieces. Lot of John Does in them days."

Tomás leaned over and whispered, "they are trying to frighten us. Act brave Felix. We are not in Guatemala. We have rights."

"Don't be so sure of that La Bamba," sour face said.

And Felix hadn't been sure of it either. Fear had at last begun to make a permanent hollow in his heart. But no more was said.

It was relief he felt when he saw the sign for the interstate leading back to the city, and was assured enough that there would be no alligators.

They finally arrived at the station on Tulane, where the squad car came to rest. For a few minutes, the police officers both left the car and entered the building. Once they were out of sight, Tomás leaned over and asked Felix if he could reach into his coat pocket.

"They did not take my phone," the old man said, "they must have forgotten."

Felix, with his hands behind his back, scooted up against his friend, who lowered himself down and guided his jacket pocket over Felix's grasping fingers. He then instructed

Felix, who could not see the phone's screen, how to find the buttons that dialed Mrs. Herbert.

She didn't answer, but as the cops reemerged from the building and began walking towards the cruiser, there was just enough time to leave one, brief, whispered message.

"Felix and I arrested by bad cops. HELP! Tulane Station."

There was no time to put the phone back, and so Tomás used his thigh to push it onto the floor. Then the two were led into the station in cuffs and marched right past the booking desk. As Felix was escorted through that waiting room, filled up with tense, waiting spouses and night-shift lawyers, a man in a fedora stopped mid gait and stared at him. They locked eyes with each other in an auspicious moment.

Chapter 12

The man who had just spotted Felix in the lobby was Detective Melancon, a man who had lately been seeing plenty of Felix's face in pictures of a happy family. The recognition was instant. This was a face on his to do list, one item in a thick folder of loose ends concerning a case that the detective hadn't been able, in good conscience, to close.

First of all, the guy, Robert. He didn't hit any of the usual points of a suicide. No prior attempts or records of any mental health issues. Solid family life. Three dependents. Wealthy with a good job. A man of books and science with a strong hold on the world. Active in Carnival. A carouser but not a drunk. And on top of all that he, what, decides that he is going to go crawl under a train? A medical doctor? A man of science like this and he can't come up with a more humane way to take himself out than to kneel down on some tracks late at night and turn himself into sushi?

Then you have the family. The mother and the wife. The kids. And now the brother in the flesh. All of these people who look up to this big capable doctor. They all have to be asked questions, followed up with. In the months leading up to his death, this man lets slip no dark utterances, no doubts about his reasons to live? He spends no nights hiding in some dive, pursues no new woman. Instead he heals and cures and eats and sleeps just the same as he had been doing for years. Then he crawls under a damn train on *one* dark night of the soul?

It didn't work for Melancon, but he hadn't really been able to come up with any better ideas. He had a lot of questions left to ask. And in walks this kid straight from out of his file and into real life. Is dragged in, more like it. Sometimes you do catch a bit of luck out of left field.

The detective walked up to the counter, to Janine.

"Hey there."

"The hell you want Melancon?"

He thought about it for a second, "Well, you could start by admitting that you resent me. Probably because you peg me as some sort of narcissist, which…is likely due to the fact that we slept together but that the relationship started going cold soon after that due to my inability to…"

"You talk too much," Janine said, and averted her big lovely eyes to some paperwork.

"There is a second thing I want."

"I'm incredulous…"

Melancon lowered his voice. "That kid and the dark skinned man, the two that just passed through here, what were they booked for?"

"I don't know who you are talking about."

"You know, they just came through here. The two men in suits with Earl and Smith?"

She waved her hands at the paperwork covering her desk. "I told you, if they're here they ain't been booked."

"That strikes me as strange."

"Yeah I don't really care how it strikes you. I'm in the weeds here."

Melancon stared at her.

"Could it be that your hostility is a deep cover for unresolved feelings? Or perhaps that…"

"Fuck off."

And so he fucked off. But it was sincerely strange, the feeling he'd had seeing the kid. Unaccountably odd. And why hadn't they been booked into the system? Melancon's curiosity would have to be satisfied.

Which is how he found himself to be gently rapping at the door of IR number four.

First and foremost, he knew what he was getting himself into. That is, Melancon knew a crooked cop when he saw one, and Smith and Earl were two of the crookedest cops he had ever seen. The issue was that Melancon had opened his mouth to both of them, and so they knew that *he knew* they were crooked. This meant that these two dimwits carefully avoided any and all proximity to Melancon whenever they could help it. When they couldn't, they were apt to lower their voices when he came in the breakroom, take the stairs when he took the elevator, and shrewdly (for them) avoided playing on his team at the department picnic kickball game.

So, his suspicions were already aroused. Which is why when Earl cracked the door a few inches, and told Melancon to take a walk, the detective noticed that the little red light, the one that always flickers from the corner of all interrogation rooms during questioning, beaming like torches of legitimacy, had, in the case of interrogation room number four, been snuffed out.

The detective felt that this gave him license to be a bit insistent. He knocked again.

This time, red faced Smith came to the door.

"Jesus Christ Melancon, this don't concern you."

"Considering I'm a detective and you are ostensibly a beat cop, what makes you think you can use the interrogation room? Secondly, are you aware that this is not, in fact, a television show and you having the camera off is a serious breach of protocol…and third…"

"What are you, threatening us? You going to rat us out or what?"

Melancon considered this a moment. "Absolutely. Not only will I report you myself regarding this specific occasion, I'll also report you on the bribe you took in April, on Earl's solicitation of prostitutes, on the…"

"For fuck sake," Earl said, coming to the door. "We just in here talking, but fine. What do you want?"

"Leave the room," Melancon said, and gave them a cold look.

They pair of cops looked at each other tensely.

"Five minutes," Earl said, and the two filed out like sullen children.

Melancon flicked on the camera. He pressed the button on the recorder, and sat down across from the two. He made a mental note of all the bruises on the brother's face.

"What in the name of Christ is going on here gentlemen?" Melancon asked, once the room was arranged. He pulled a pen out of his shirt pocket.

Felix and Tomás looked at each other. Felix's face was beginning to swell, and this made him appear dubious and angry. Unless, of course, he actually was dubious and angry. There was no to way tell, Melancon noted.

"We demand a lawyer," Tomás said. "I don't believe we have been charged with anything, and I believe habeas corpus…"

"Whoa whoa whoa. See this is not even an interrogation guys. You weren't booked, so what I'm concerned with is these two cops. They are on trial here, not you. I'm just wondering what they dragged you in for."

Melancon studied Felix's wounded face. The boy was silent and the air in the room smelled like fear— that spinach and shit smell the detective knew well.

So he tried another track.

"You see, I'm actually the detective that is investigating the death of your brother, Robert."

"I..." the boy looked surprised. "It's...still being investigated? I thought it was ruled a suicide."

Melancon raised his eyebrows at the young man, flicked and twirled the pen in his hands a few times, and said, "I don't believe that your brother committed suicide. From your expression I take it you aren't so convinced yourself. There was no reason for him to do so, no history of mental illness, no gambling debts. Rich doctors with beautiful families who live uptown don't just jump under trains. Unless there is something that your family, or you, can tell me about Robert's state of mind, then yes, the investigation is still open. Officially."

"So." Felix put his palms down on the table and slid closer in to the detective. "What you are saying....Mr..."

"Detective Melancon."

"So you're saying you think Robert could have been murdered?"

"Well, I haven't gotten there yet. Right now, I'm still trying to rule out the possibility that maybe he lost a contact lens on the train track and was trying to find it."

"Robert didn't wear contacts."

"Well there you go, scratch that theory. Got any others?"

"I think I have figured some things out," Felix blurted. The old Latin man put a quick hand on his charge's forearm, as if to say *be careful*, but the boy's face said he wanted to talk.

The detective leaned back, put the pen between his teeth, and said, "Alright, let's hear your theory gumshoe."

"It's going to sound crazy."

"Well, are you crazy?"

"I don't think so."

Felix looked around uncomfortably, nibbled at his hand, which was taped up and leaking blood onto the interrogation table, his knife wound having reopened in the scuffle.

"Do you know about the angel corkscrew mask?"

"The what now?" Melancon said, his eyes narrowing.

Felix cleared his throat. "I have reason to believe...I believe that my brother may have been involved with some bad doctors. Specifically the Krewe of Asclepius. More specifically, the Troxclair family. I think that maybe they had something to do with Robert's death."

The clicking pen stopped and Melancon looked up at him.

Felix seemed to be inflating.

"And you say you're not crazy?" Melancon asked, craning his neck at the odd young man, peering down at him, wrinkling his chin at him.

"No, he is not crazy," Tomás said deliberately, and looked down his nose at the detective. Felix smiled his swollen grin through cracked lips.

"You are his…" Melancon twirled his pen at the old man.

"His butler. His friend. Tomás De Valencia. I raised him from a baby."

The detective nodded, then leaned forward and whispered to the both of them.

"Drugs?"

"No…not…not anymore," Felix stammered out.

"Well. In that case, I suppose all you need is some evidence. Go ahead and present it if you have any. I mean, now that we've established that you aren't crazy and you aren't on drugs, I suppose anything is admissible."

Tomás made a fist, lightly tapping the table. "We were arrested, in the process of gathering evidence, by your officers. These Troxclair, they assaulted Felix."

"I took a picture. She had drawers full of heavy opiate pharms. But her goons took my cell phone."

Melancon looked at Felix. "So, you are on drugs then?"

Tomás gasped, exasperated. "He was assaulted… you can see the bruises…this is the… ¿qué es? …the, what do you call it, the infliction of bodily harm."

"Oh, so we have a lawyer and a detective here. Quite the tag team."

"Are you going to help us or sit here and practice your witty banter?" Felix asked.

Melancon sighed. "Look...what I see here is a young guy who's just been through some trauma, is now desperate to prove that he is not just a rich silver-spoon type, and sees what he thinks is an opportunity to get revenge. Revenge for someone he just lost under somewhat sketchy circumstances, sure. His brain has been clouded by drugs, and his sheltered lifestyle's got him thinking that life is one big black and white detective film. On top of that, you have this guy who has been the family confidant for years, now enabling you in your quest for revenge, because he is so deeply on your side that he wouldn't dream of doing otherwise. Even if you *were* flat out wrong. Am I getting close here?"

It hit Felix in the chest. Why did they call it being "blunt" anyway? It was more like a knife than a club. Sharp and precise stabbing rather than a wild crushing. For a moment the detective's words hung in the air. Silence.

Felix stood up, an even more angry expression settling over his battered face.

"And you? Being perceptive doesn't make you any less of an asshole. You know that right? But what you don't know is *me*. Everyone just assumes it. They take one fucking look at me and figure they've read my whole life story in paperback. But you haven't. You don't know anything about me, my brother, or Tomás here. You write whatever story you want, just like everybody else. I don't care if you are going to help us or not. But I'm going to figure this thing out, and if I die trying, well that will just be something you'll have to live with. And you can spend your time psychoanalyzing yourself when that day comes. But I can tell you what's true, and that is I've been chased by a black Plymouth, I've been threatened with swamp death by crooked cops, I've been beaten up by a hunchback's entourage, but this has been the worst insult of all. To sit here and have some dickhead assume he has me all figured out within five minutes of meeting me…and another thing…"

"Did you say… a black Plymouth?"

Felix lost his momentum. "That's right."

The detective scratched his chin, tugged at his bowtie.

Felix's accusatory tone softened. "What? What is it?"

"It's just that. There has been a black Plymouth showing up everywhere I go. At the drugstore, on my way to work, when I go out on the porch for my morning coffee. I thought I was just getting old and paranoid but…"

"Looks like they're on to you too, Detective," Tomás said with a smirk.

"Ok…Let's not get into too many *'theys'* here guys, not just yet, that's how these things get out of control. I tell you what, how about you stop playing Don Quixote and Sancho for a bit and let me look into this thing."

"I'll never agree to that. I have to fight this battle for my brother. I won't stop just because you say so." Felix said.

"I kinda figured."

"I don't trust you," Felix said, with his eyebrows raised.

"You'd be wise not to do too much trusting at the moment, I'd wager," The detective shot back.

Just then there was a knock on the door.

"Fuck off Earl, before I call the Chief."

But it was Janine.

"Kids mom is here, and she's pissed," Janine said.

"Got a lawyer with her?" Melancon asked over his shoulder.

"I'd bet she has a whole team of lawyers, just to look at her."

Melancon tilted his head at the two and nodded them out towards the exit.

"Take a vacation guys. Use all that money you've got for God sake. A trip to Thailand or something. Let the professionals sort this out."

Then he looked at Felix in the eyes.

"You've got my word on this one, young man. I'll keep it open."

Chapter 13

They waited for her to speak, but out in the parking lot Mrs. Herbert quietly handed the keys to over to Tomás and said nothing. Felix was half expecting her to yell, or express disbelief, to ask where the Continental was, to ask one of a thousand questions begged here and now. But she didn't, and he felt troubled when she didn't ask or reprove or demand, but instead slipped on a pair of sunglasses, hiding herself in the night. There was a slackness to her which was unusual, and it worried him to think what secret fire might be fizzling out inside her.

Once they were down the street, safely away from the station, she wrapped herself in a scarf and lit a cigarette. There was a smell in the car like wine and burnt toast, like she'd tried her hand at cooking and given up for a bottle. Felix turned and looked out of the back window, nervous for signs of the black Plymouth, or maybe even a police car, but found an empty roadway. His muscles relaxed and he realized how exhausted he was, how severely his face and stomach were bruised by his run in with Lena Troxclair.

"We are lucky Tomás."

"Yes." He let out a long breath and ran his hands down to the base of the steering wheel. After a pause: "I will call a tow truck for the Continental. As for your cellphone, I'm afraid I'll have to simply order you a new one."

Then he looked at her in the rear view mirror.

"Your son was very brave Madame. Very brave."

Her eyebrows rose and fell behind the dark glasses. Silence. Felix was having a difficult time keeping his head up, bobbing a few times with heavy sleep. All the adrenaline, all the nerves, everything was crashing down at last.

When he had almost faded out, she spoke.

"I don't want to know the details of what you two have been up to."

He jerked awake, caught Tomás' eyes in the rearview.

"Do I?" she said, harder this time. She leaned forward, swaying. The curls she usually wore in her hair had straightened, and the lines in her face ran long and deep. They'd driven onto a bad road now and began to bounce in unison.

"Mother... you don't honestly believe that Robert committed suicide, do you?"

A deep pothole rocked the car just then and her body gave in to the punch of gravity, wobbling a moment too long before she was able to steady herself against the passenger seat in front of her. "I'm not…ready to…examine that question Felix. He is dead. My son is dead. That is about *all* I can fit into my head right now. Do you understand that?"

They waited through another block of the heavy silence. Tomás tried to roll up the privacy blind which separated the cab from the back, but Mrs. Herbert put a hand out to show that she wanted it to remain open.

"I know you have something to prove here, Felix. You always have had that. But I really, really wish you would stop it. I wish you would let it rest, son. Because there is only one thing you need to prove here, one thing only, at least to me. Put on a business suit, dry yourself off, go to work every morning like a normal man. There is that corner office, down at the plant, just sitting empty, waiting for you all this time. You could wear a suit and tie, and if you didn't look good in the suit so what? You'd find your color. You'd grow into it. It doesn't matter. I know what you are worried about. You are worried you won't be good at it. But the secret is, you don't really *need* to be good at anything. It is more like you need to be there, if you understand me. But I know you're worried…"

She hiccupped, and then laughed at herself, or at him.

"Worried that you won't be able to hack it in a normal life. And if you were no good at it at first then so what? That's up to you. But it's the thing you could do. If you wanted to get better at things, you'd get better. Then you'd get married and have children and you'd name your first boy Robert."

Her hands were dancing in front of her now, conducting his could-be life. "You'd buy a house somewhere across town. Then you'd live on and on and on until you got old like me. Like your father."

More sad laughter, choked out in sobs that sent her into a coughing fit. She threw her cigarette out the window. Dark oak trees flashed by outside and the road leveled out again.

"But I know that isn't you Felix. Because I know *precisely* who you are. You are too restless. All of your problems come from your inability to just sit quietly in a room by yourself for a while. You've been that way since you were a child. Robert, he would sit and play with a toy for hours. Just one toy. He'd treasure it, figure out all its secrets and mechanisms. Appreciate it so deeply. That one toy would keep him busy for hours and hours. But you would wander outside into the garden, try to climb into the fountain— then you would break your toys and cry that they were broken. I know you are never going to sit still Felix, but I'm asking you to drop this... revenge thing, or whatever it is. For me. I'm old. I'm tired, and most of all I'm terribly heartbroken. My son is dead. It is going to take me a while before I'll be able to do any thinking about that. I don't need *what ifs* in the middle of the night. And I certainly don't need to pick you up from jail at three in the morning."

She smiled tightly out at the dark trees, a contortion, a grimace. Who could know what was going on behind those thick sunglasses? Again, she leaned forward. "And what do you have to say Tomás. You selfless person. What part do you play in these capers, my old sweet man? Did he put you up to it? Or have you been stoking these flames all along?"

She reached out to touch him, but seemed to think better of it. Tomás shifted uncomfortably in his seat and put on his blinker to turn off St. Charles into their driveway. He nodded into the mirror. "We were only searching for the truth, Madame. The truth cannot wait for anything, or anyone."

"I know you were only doing what you thought was right. But the *truth* isn't going to put those pieces of Robert back together. It isn't going to put the blood back into his veins. So, with that in mind, please, the both of you see that you let my son rest in peace," she said.

"Yes Madame."

She looked at Felix.

"Promise me son."

He hesitated, feeling the thump of his heartbeat.

"I promise. I won't look for trouble Mama. But just so you know. I believe it is probably too late to step out of things at this point. The trouble is already in our backyard."

She nodded. "Well, when that time comes, we will decide what to do. For now, I need a drink," she said, fishing in her purse for another cigarette.

Tomás dropped them off under the carport, hurrying around to open the door for Felix's mother. The air was crisp and cold.

"How's Dad?"

"Go see for yourself. He's actually mentioned your name a few times lately. Hasn't said a word about Robert."

"He understands more than he lets on," said Felix.

"Poor old creature."

He wanted only to sleep, but sleep wouldn't come. After a shower, some coffee, and a change of clothes, he made his way up the long staircase to his father's study. The sun had risen and cast long squares of sunlight into the great empty spaces of the house. He knocked on the door, just as a formality, just out of respect for a lifelong habit. There was no sense in waiting to be invited in.

His father was seated in his wheelchair looking out through a bay window, watching a blue jay dance and bluster across the yard. Below, in the garden, a man was finishing the last steps towards ridding the estate of any and all Carnival decorations, leaving the yard sparse and empty before its time. The brown lawn was ready to mourn now – the rolls of purple string lights lay bundled on the oak roots, the large grinning masks stacked leaning against the shed. The ribbons and beads were strewn on the grass where they had been chased out of the boughs.

"Dad. I need a gun."

His father noticed him and stiffened in his chair, as if insulted. "Of course, of course. Why not have a gun? Only, be warned my boy: If a gun appears in the first act, it absolutely must go off by the third act. It's a dramatic principle my boy. You understand."

"Yeah Dad, I understand that."

He had knocked, and he had asked. But Felix knew where it rested. He'd known always, in fact. It wasn't "*a* gun" so much as it was "*the* gun". The only gun he had ever held, ever fired. He'd grown up with the gun glowing there in the second drawer from the bottom, right side, behind the envelopes and checkbooks. It was kept in a leather holster, behind the magnifying glass and the letter opener, long and metal and hard as manhood itself.

He found it now as it ever was, all chambers except the first one full of expandable hollow-point bullets. Safety on. Leather holster strap sensibly checking the firing mechanism. Safe, but waiting as all tools wait for its purpose. Felix weighed it in his hand.

".38 special," he said to his father. "I never did understand what was so special about it."

"It was the light, it was the dark," the old man mumbled, nodding towards the pistol where it lay flat in his son's hand.

"Well let's hope it doesn't end like that story, eh Pop?"

"There is no end to the story," he said.

Felix stuffed the weapon into his right pocket and leaned down to eye level with his father. "What would you have done, in this situation? I wonder. How would you have found these people out? Would you have taken the thing in your own hands? Hired someone? Or buried yourself in work, instead?"

"It is impossible to suffer, without making someone pay for it," the old man said, clearly affronted somehow at the precociousness of his remaining son.

The old line stirred up memories of long gone talks with his father, of lectures he had been forced to undergo in this very room. It was an after-school ritual— when Felix had been more concerned with basketball and girls, his father had sat him down and force-fed him Nietzsche.

"I wish I'd paid a bit more attention," Felix said to the universe of books surrounding him. The leather bindings with their gold flake letters had begun to grow dusty. "Maybe it would have made it easier to get into your head these days. I don't know what to do."

The service doorbell rang downstairs, and they could hear Tomás' reassuring tread crossing the marble floor of the entryway.

"Let's talk later, Dad."

Felix was halfway down the stairs when Tomás cleared his throat from the threshold.

"Madame, the workmen have finished removing all trace of decoration, as you've asked. Will there be anything else?"

"Just write them a check please," Felix's mother choked out.

Tomás walked over to her and, in a slightly lower voice said: "They also asked if we wish to remove the remote security camera from the oak, Madame."

"What camera are you talking about Tomás?" Felix called down from the stairs.

He turned to them both and cleared his throat once more, saying in a loud, official voice, "It seems the trouble has been in our back yard for some time already."

Chapter 14

It lay there on the coffee table for a great while and his mother had stopped her drinking entirely, to glare at it more severely, perhaps.

A little shell, textured as if by hand— someone had mottled its fine black carapace with paint the same color as a St. Charles oak bough. She looked at it with that face a woman gets, with that scowl for when a water bug is found crawling through the parlor, that worm writhing across her foot, or that spider dipping into her bathwater. That is to say the creature on the coffee table was a startling offense, an invader, and her face reflected new and harrowing degrees of unwelcome as she sat regarding the tiny camera for the better part of an hour.

Felix resisted every impulse to exclaim that he'd "told her so" or some variant thereof. He waited with the patience of the righteous, standing off behind her, near the window, searching the branches for more evidence of what had come upon his family.

She'd sat scrunch-faced for a long while and then looked at him and said that she was sorry.

"I absolve you from your promise Felix," she'd said. Her voice was clear and sober.

"But, that doesn't mean I want you to be involved in this."

"What *does* that mean mother?"

"It means that instead of forcing you to stop, I'm going to let you choose to stop. Because clearly, whatever this is it is beyond us. We aren't violent people Felix. We don't "bug" our enemies, or get them fired, or have any police officers in our pockets as you describe. So, there is simply nothing else for it. I'm going to offer you and Tomás a vacation. Anywhere in the world you want to go, on me. So that you can get the hell away from all of this. At least until the heat dies down."

It hurt him to hear that his mother thought the task beyond him. She knew him, after all, like no one else on earth. She'd even said so herself in the car. If she thought he couldn't do it, well, perhaps he could not after all. Perhaps acting brave wasn't being brave in the end. Rather, it was something intrinsic, like a birth mark or a beautiful singing voice; you could only pretend to be a hero for so long before you got yourself in water far over your head, and then the water plugged up your lungs because pretending to be a good swimmer was not enough to keep you buoyant.

"What about you? What are you going to do, mother?"

"First I'm going to call a very serious man I know who runs a private security firm. I'm going to call him and I'm going to have him send over some burly fellows with sunglasses on who never smile. That's right I'm going to hire a couple men in black suits to keep me company. Then I'm going to lock the doors of this house for a month. I'm going to take up a hobby. Pottery or glassblowing maybe? I'll get one of my friends on Julia Street to grant me some kind of exhibition in the summer. That's it. I'm going to spend a month working with my hands and staying in. I'm going to let all of this cool down. Lose myself for a while, from the comfort of my own home. Drink and create and sleep. That's all. And when you and Tomás get back, I'm going to watch a slideshow of you two riding camels near the Pyramids, or hiking along the Great Wall, or whatever it is you do in Guatemala. From there we will see what can be done."

Felix walked from the window to where his mother was sitting on the couch. He put his hand on her shoulder, standing behind her.

"And if I refuse to go?" He asked.

"Then you refuse to go."

"Give me some time to think about it."

"You've never been one to take time to think about things, Felix. But do what you feel you need to."

So he did. Felix lingered around the house, had a long dreamless nap, and found himself that evening sitting on the upper balcony that overlooked St. Charles Avenue as the city began its long slide into Carnival. Tomás sat next to him nursing an iced tea.

It was perhaps one of the loveliest streets in the entire world at sunset, but the February build-up was an odd time for it. The fireflies were all gone. The streetcars were put away in the tin-roofed warehouse, and territory was marked. The neutral ground became less neutral, and with the coolers and ladders invading every patch of grass, small conflicts began. It was a fight as old as time, over land and space and the rights and rules regarding them, with spray-painted amateur surveys and tussles over disputed earth. The traffic was blockaded. Then the Avenue waited.

Thirty minutes late the thump and glint of brass came lilting over the crowd, echoing down the long tunnel of trees. The clack of Clydesdales and the growl of tractors followed close behind, and it was Carnival.

"I don't know Tomás. Maybe we should do what they both said, my mom and that detective. Buy a ticket someplace. Skip out on all this and give things a little while to cool down. I've seen enough Mardi Gras shit to last a lifetime anyway."

Tomás placed his tea on the table, folded his hands in his lap and looked down at them.

"I mean, this is dangerous right? We are saying…we are going on the assumption that they fucking killed Robert. Like, somehow they managed to force him to bisect himself. Think about that for a minute. Don't you feel the fear? We really can't step up to people like that, can we?"

Tomás fingered the condensation on his tea glass and looked out over the Avenue.

"Why are you helping me, anyway, Tomás? You know you don't have to help me. I don't know what my mom pays you but I'm sure it isn't enough to get tangled up with these people."

Tomás took a long breath. The parade was getting closer and the crowded streets were falling into formation, pressing against an invisible barrier towards where the floats would roll.

"I believe it is time I told you a sad story, Felix."

"You never tell stories Tomás," Felix said quietly. "But I'd love to hear anything you have to say, sad or not."

"One hopes to keep a professional distance in these matters, Felix," the old man said and turned his head towards his friend.

Felix waved away his concern. "Don't be ridiculous old man. You are one of the only people in the world I can trust right now."

Tomás nodded, smiling, and began. "My brother was named Eme," he said.

"I didn't know you had a brother, Tomás."

"None of your family knows this. In fact, I don't believe I have spoken of Eme since I left Guatemala in ninety-five."

"Older?"

"He was my younger brother, quite a grave and serious person for his age. Some of us thought he could grow up to be something very serious. A general or something like this. He had a…revolutionary spirit. Fiery but… ¿qué es?…I believe the word is *conscientious*."

Felix waited, pictured a graver, younger, more serious version of Tomás, found it impossible.

"Our father was a metal worker. Highly skilled. He owned his own storefront in Escuintla, where I was born. He was a self-made man, much like your own father is."

"Was," Felix said.

"Well, at least he is living still. My own father has been dead for a dozen years now."

A drunk man was screaming on the street below, he twirled around, lost balance and fell over into a mound of beads.

"Many times my father would leave my brother and I in charge of the store, in order to visit some wealthy person's manor, to see about the iron railing, to give estimates on lamp repair, to shake hands with his customers, you see."

The first floats could now be seen in the distance, a giant snake coming out of the trees, a blossom of wild color. The fat brass thundered and snarled, closer now.

"I regret to say that I was not very interested in my father's business at the time. I often left the running of the store to Eme, who some might say took it a bit too seriously. One day he caught a thief in the store, a boy, not much younger than he was at the time. The boy had come in through the back door and was loading our tools into a truck. Of course, when Eme saw this he immediately confronted the boy. According to the one old woman, who saw this taking place across the street, a man with an eyepatch got out of the cab of the truck and fired three bullets into Eme, before ordering the boy to continue loading the tools."

"Tomás ….Jesus."

He pulled a white handkerchief from his coat pocket, and as the parade began in earnest, Tomás wiped away a tear.

"I thought for a long time about trying to find this man with the truck. But my family, and…we never had the resources like your family does Felix. Like you do. We were just tradesmen. But you have a chance. You don't want to live with the feeling of having had this chance and walking away from it. I know you Felix. You are a man of honor. You are lacking in skill and confidence, but you cannot help that. It will come with time. But more importantly, you are naïve and believe far too deeply in fairness. I find this is a particularly American weakness. The idea that things are ever fair. But in the end, it doesn't have to be a fair fight. It just has to be a fight."

There was a long spell of silence on the porch, but the roar below grew louder.

Felix shook his head. "I don't know what to say."

Tomás stood up and crossed the length of the porch. The speakers were tremendous now, all sorts of different music playing at once.

"Say no to your Mother's offer," he said, and went back inside the house.

The marching bands rolled. The flambeaux danced and skipped and wailed for quarters. The cymbals clashed and the horsemen hailed the growing crowd. Felix still had the gun in his pocket. His head was so clear now, calm and bright. He thought deeply about his friend, the long lost little boy, and the man with the eye patch. All from a far off time and place but as real as the tear he'd seen fall into the white handkerchief. He imagined carrying this new knowledge off someplace, flying away with it to go lie in a hammock on some alien shore. His brain would torment him, would remind him of this very moment, and the way he had tucked the gun back in the drawer and quietly booked two tickets online to someplace he couldn't pronounce. And to force Tomás to go with him? It would only remind his friend of the brave little brother Eme with the gunshots in his chest. The man in the truck driving away to live his new, slightly enriched life. It would remind him that he had surrendered to unfairness. And that would be who he was for the rest of his life. The choice he was facing really wasn't a choice at all, he decided.

The parade passed, and Felix sat for another hour watching its halting progress. Behind the final float, garbage trucks and street sweepers arrived to scrape the Avenue clean of revelry. There was nothing left of the chaos but a big mess and another cold front blowing in through the leaves

Felix knocked on the butler chamber window, which looked out onto this upper porch.

Tomás opened it immediately.

"This Krewe of doctors. This, 'Asclepius'. When does their Krewe roll?"

Tomás beamed from within his darkened chamber.

"Acting brave is being brave, Felix," the old man said.

Chapter 15

The Krewe of Asclepius rolled the very next night, its first parade in recent history, and followed that well-worn St. Charles route that passed right in front of the Herbert family estate.

He hadn't been back to his apartment. It felt like nothing more now than a desolate, poorly-carpeted place to die. He couldn't go back there with his jigsaws and TV dinners and wait for them to come. The thought of sleeping alone, with nothing but a four digit code between him and these figures, was enough to dry up his courage. Dreams of them coming in the night— dark, masked faces, serpents around a sharpened staff. If they were going to come for him, let them do it with witnesses; there might be safety in numbers.

So he remained with his family on the Avenue. His mother had made calls, and a man now sat on their porch or in their living room. Just as she'd said he would be, the man was dark-suited, straight-faced, and didn't say much to any of them. Felix wasn't sure what good this man would do if it came down to it, but it made his Mother feel better, and it had added a few hours to his sleep that morning as well.

He was glad to be at home again. He wanted to be with Tomás anyway, to put heads together, form plans, to hear his mother's ice cubes tinkling in her gin glass. Even more so he needed to be able to pass this time without dwelling. Dwelling brought the fear, and so Felix even found himself sitting in his father's study for long hours waiting for the old man's next muddled excerpt, and reading aloud when the mood came to him.

That morning, Treasure Island caught his eye. Noting how his father's eyes would glisten during the exciting bits, the rapier fights and cannon blasts, how he would rock in his chair when Long John appeared, Felix kept on with the story.

It allowed him to forget for a while, to still frazzled nerves and quell the anxiety rising up over the evening's coming parade. Right by his front door it would come, King and Queen at the front, all their minions and attendants dancing in costume. Those twin snakes of the angel corkscrew would be hovering somewhere in papier-mâché.

And he'd have to face it, to hide in an apple barrel and suss out what he could.

The day passed slowly with ships and gold and peg legs. Tomás mostly remained in his room aside from bringing food out, that same late breakfast he'd been making Mrs. Herbert for years and years: two grapefruit halves and two slices of wheat toast with strawberry jam. She took it in the study with them and sat and listened while she slowly ate. But her face, even during the more exciting bits, remained dubious and uncertain, as if she had half expected something less frivolous to come out of the book. Or out of her son, perhaps. Felix thought his mother must reserve her creative, adventurous energies for other things, for the roping in of tears or the brushing of her husband's white hair, for all that promised pottery or glass blowing or whatever. Her powers remained a mystery as always. She wasn't like the Jim Hawkins or the Billy Bones, obvious in their intrepid virtues, impressed with maps and baubles and strong arms. She was more like the sea itself.

He read the whole book aloud and it took him nearly five hours.

By the end of it he had a light supper and sat on the upstairs balcony again. Tomás' window was open and Latin music could be heard from his chamber. Always it was "corazon" this and "corazon" that. The heart. The organ. The central item. Felix felt his own had aged ten years in the last week, working so hard, thumping in a frenzy.

The parade was due at seven. The revelers had long since arrived and begun drinking in the streets, grilling, tossing footballs and frisbees in the last remaining slivers of sunlight.

He checked the chambers of the pistol for the twentieth time. If only it was as simple to check his own resolve. Open up the chambers and look inside at the hard lead, a heart made of cast-iron and gunpowder. It wasn't that he planned to use the pistol that night— to assassinate a doctor at

Carnival, under the eyes of half the city, wouldn't be advisable no matter how effective a revenge it might have been. No, Felix checked and rechecked the pistol because he wanted to know to absolute assuredness that, should the need arise, he wouldn't be left helpless, without claws.

And so, with the grunting of the tractors bouncing down the tree trunks, Tomás came out of his room and stood at the top of the stairs, two delicate carnival masks held out in his open palms. One enchanted, jubilant, delighted; the second pained, stark, and unfulfilled.

"Which one do you want, Felix?" Tomás asked.

"I wasn't planning on wearing a costume," Felix admitted, and put his hand out for happiness.

They walked out onto the street and into a glad chaos. Children ran between their knees and a grown man staggered from side to side, raising a handful of neon ropes above his head. Smells of beer and urine, hotdogs and diesel fumes. Under the screaming and laughter and tractor engines, the wail of horns and the smack of hooves, Tomás leaned over and whispered in Felix's ear. "What exactly do you have planned for this, Felix?"

"I'm just here for the beads," he said, and let his mask beam back at his friend. But inside, behind the thick, colored plastic, his eyes were darting from side to side. *Just what do I have planned?*

He just needed to face them. To know that he could face them. To let them pass right by his home and cower within would be too much to bear. And, with a bit of serendipity, maybe he would glean some other detail from the frivolity.

Tomás' head turned, and the old man's gaze went cold. There they were: the inaugural King and Queen of the Krewe of Asclepius. The first float was rolling towards them with all the speed of farm equipment. Closer and closer. A wide row of pearly teeth, grinning beneath a plastic mask. A drink of something rested on the railing in front of his Highness as he bent down to tear open a bag of throws, plastic trinkets fresh from Shanghai no doubt, that he would rain down on the masses for the next several hours.

The King was masked— just his eyes. The bottom half of his face was clear. It didn't matter— his long body and curly hair was a dead giveaway for Max Troxclair. He was wearing a gold toga with some sort of fiber optic frills woven into the fabric, a caduceus staff held aloft and waving at the happy revelers.

Next to him was the unmistakably hunched figure of Lena Troxclair, in similar dress but with a far zestier wave than her husband. She bowed to the crowd, throwing kisses at children and waving the tail of her toga behind her.

After the royal float was another full of their court attendants. This float stopped in front of Felix for a moment, and he read the signboard. "Paean, Physician of the Gods." It contained more toga sporting elites proffering baubles to the groping masses. A toy landed by Felix's feet.

It was a plush filled with cotton, stitched together in some sweatshop, and sporting the same snakes around a sharp staff as he had begun to see everywhere, now. The angel corkscrew. The only difference was that at the bottom in big, friendly, purple letters the word "Scopodol" was written.

Advertising, at least overt advertising, on floats and Mardi Gras regalia was not a thing that was generally done in Felix's Carnival experience, which was rather extensive. He picked the toy up so Tomás could read it also.

But before they could discuss it any further, the engine on the lead tractor lurched to life and the floats began their slow progress down the Avenue once again.

"Let's follow the Troxclairs," Felix said.

And so, with Tomás trailing behind, he began ducking his way through the crowd. He dodged beads and cups, rubber balls and light up roses, drunks and children. The crowd pressed him in, but still Felix pushed his way through, squirming to follow the lead float. To keep track of it, he watched the caduceus staff flutter in the air, observed the gilded hunch of Lena Troxclair swaying under the oak canopies. He continued on for block after block, headed towards downtown where the crowds grew only thicker.

At a chokepoint near a port-o-john, Felix had to squeeze through a thick row of bodies. When he came out the other side he looked back for Tomás. But his friend was gone, blocked by the crowd perhaps. Felix considered, just for a moment, going back homewards. But the King and Queen were inching further away, and he felt a deep pull to see them as they were, basking themselves in the glory of the moment.

It might reveal some weakness, some chink in the armor, and Felix needed to be there when the unmasking took place.

Another part of him wanted to show himself. To rip off his mask and yell, "I see you," for all of Carnival to hear. He wanted Lena and Max to know they were being watched, followed, tracked— that they weren't the only ones with eyes in the trees. And here they were no longer in their grand estate in Spanish Turn, where they could calmly pick up a receiver and have Felix removed. Here there was chaos. Murderous, pistol-bearing chaos come to ruin their moment in the sun.

Here was revenge.

He pushed and shoved now, elbowing children and running over the feet of old women. The masks danced in the streetlamp above him, laughing, bouncing, each of them branded with a glowing caduceus on the forehead. The King and Queen of blood. The Gods of murder. A royal family of base assassins. Here they were to behold. The crowd only groveled at their feet.

The music grew louder and he lost the float, regained it, lost it, and regained it again. They were falling away from him, inch by inch.

Then, in a clearing where the crowd had parted, it hit him square in the face. A plush throw, just like all the others. It was soft, fluffy, and sewn together in that same fake Chinese leather, filled with that same fluffy, cotton-like substance. It bounced off his forehead and fell into his hands. He looked down.

It was a plush train: "Scopodol" in big black smoke letters on side of the engine.

He raised his head, and there they were, not ten feet away from him and stopped now. The King and Queen regarded him and their tractor hushed. His clearing receded; the crowd lunged forward at the halt, groping, grabbing, yelling, laughing, dancing and raising their arms on high as if to some great hunchbacked deity. But the two doctors had stopped throwing for the moment. Both of them looked directly at Felix, who stood there dumbfounded, with a plush train in his hands, trying his hardest not to wither. The world spun, the oak limbs grew fingers and they reached out towards Felix. The bones of fingers, of the dead, and the crushing weight of the beads hanging in their thin, wooden digits threatened to shake loose from their foundation with all else of worth and value, to drop everything precious in a hot moment, just as Robert had done, or been forced to do.

Felix took a step towards the lead float, raised his head high to the King and Queen.

Acting brave is being brave.

"Did you kill my brother?" He yelled.

There was no reply.

"How did you do it? How could you make it all look like an accident?"

The crowd began parting now, like a river around a rock.

"Did you know that he has children? A wife, a brother?"

People were looking now, noticing. Things grew quiet in that little sphere.

"How is it that you managed to have police officers on your side?"

He inched closer, or at least, that was how he saw it. What had felt to him like a slow, confident step forward, was in reality a headlong charge towards the lead float. In his mind, he had been pointing only an accusatory finger, while the men and women and children around him saw instead a wildly brandished .38 special, its barrel glinting far brighter than any of the kitsch of Carnival ever could.

It would be hard to recall the exact details of what happened, but Felix was incredibly lucky that night. The police officer on horseback had already had a few drinks, and so was perhaps feeling charitable enough not to shoot at Felix. Or maybe he was just worried there would be an investigation, or he'd hit someone in the crowd. Secondly, because the officer on horseback had been drinking, the club he used to subdue the would-be shooter merely glanced off of the side of Felix's head, instead of cracking his skull. But it was a direct enough cuff to calm Felix's temper, and to cause him to fall to his knees and let the dizzy blackness envelop him.

Chapter 16

He awoke with a savage headache and realized he was not at home, found himself lying on more of a shelf than a bed, the left side of his face all but swollen shut and a cramping pain that lit up in his shoulder the moment he stirred.

"That was what we call a *rookie mistake*," said a male voice at the other end of the cell.

It took Felix a few moments to fully come to and see where he was, and then to think why it was that Detective Melancon looked so smug sitting on the bench across from him in this very cramped and cold jail cell.

"Really. That pain you feel in your head? Consider it the best news you've ever had. That throbbing sensation is proof that your heart is still beating. That blood still flows through your veins. Because my dear, foolish young man, cops shoot people for less than that in this city. You know that right? Happens all the time. In fact, there was a guy last week who didn't even have a gun. He was just on the lam from beating his old lady. But he made a sudden move with the wrong jumpy officer, and well... He's gone to the great hereafter."

Felix sat up and rubbed his swollen eye, thinking that this would open it, but when he felt the pain he remembered all of it. A wave of sickness washed over him. It amounted to about the worst hangover he'd ever had, all without the fun to show for it.

Melancon didn't give him any time to recover, he set right in.

"Now you are remembering. You aren't concussed, I was told medical cleared you before they stuck you in this cell, so the memory should come back crisp and clear. And right at this moment you are probably remembering and your face is heating up, your pores opening, a tingling sensation in the scalp. That's right, that's the shame you're feeling. Shame, I can only assume, not about threatening someone with a gun. You're probably feeling pretty good and right about that, considering that you believe that the people you threatened were the bad guys. The shame you feel must be about doing something so unbelievably stupid as pulling out a weapon in a crowd of people at Carnival, without even getting a shot off. I mean, if you were going to go down for this, at least get a shot off right? I still can't really figure what your game plan was here Felix. That's how you should know you did something really stupid, because I can't see a single advantage to it. And I'm pretty creative."

Felix cringed and rubbed his head. "You know you don't have to say every damn thing that pops into your head, right?"

"You know you don't have to *do* everything that pops into *your* head, right?" Melancon shot back, walking over to the edge of the cell and sticking his hands out through the bars.

Felix ran a hand through his greasy hair. "The train…they…they gave me a train."

Melancon turned back to him. "What's that kid?"

"Nothing…it was a Mardi Gras throw. They put it right into my hands…like they wanted to taunt me somehow. It said the name of a drug…you probably wouldn't believe me if I told you. Doesn't matter anyway."

Melancon sat back down and crossed his legs. He had his hands in his pocket and was looking disappointed, like maybe his horse had broken a leg during the race.

"Drug name?"

"Yeah….Scopo…something."

Melancon closed his eyes. "A train?" he said.

"Yeah, it was a plush train. Right into my hands. Like the one that killed Robert."

"Sounds like a coincidence," Melancon said.

"I thought detectives didn't believe in coincidences."

Melancon shook his head. "Too many movies kid."

"They were looking right at me, Max and Lena. Taunting me. I lost my cool. Not like I'm use to confrontations you know?"

"I don't know what the hell you are into here kid, but I've just got the sickest feeling about it. I should tell you. You should know. Officers Earl and Smith got here before me. They were just standing outside the bars looking in at you sleeping. The camera was off. They weren't saying a thing. Pretty creepy. Like maybe another ten minutes and you would have 'hung yourself by your bedsheets' or something."

"Does that stuff really happen?"

Melancon gave Felix a piercing look.

"They are working for the Troxclair's, you know, hired thugs. They know all about me and my family. They even put a hidden camera in my back yard."

Melancon blew out air. "You really think Earl and Smith are smart enough for all that? Working for Lena Troxclair, I mean how do you land a sweet gig like that? You think she is still hiring? I don't even have fucking dental. I mean, you know who she is right?"

"It's not a joke. And yes, they are doctors… and possibly murderers."

"Doctors is a bit of an understatement Felix. They are *THE* doctors. I've been doing a little looking into your dastardly nemesis. You know Lena? She showed up in town from some bumfuck place in the Florida Parishes and graduated top of her class from Tulane med. Her parents were poor Felix. Her dad worked at a goddamn Dollar General his whole life. And now here she is— on all sorts of boards and committees, a sterling record in all respects except for the one."

"What's that?"

Melancon stuck his thumbs in his trousers and put his tongue in his cheek. "Man, you are some kind of kid you know that? How did you weasel your way into this, anyway? I thought you were supposed to be off in Thailand or something by now. Don't you rich people usually run from your problems?"

Felix put his head in his hands and sighed. Then he looked back up at the detective.

"You ever lose a brother?" he asked, feeling himself warming ever so slightly to Melancon, but still holding back from showing it.

"Can't say that I have any brothers."

"Well, that makes two of us now."

There was a long pause in the conversation. They could hear doors slamming outside.

"She was investigated by the DEA back during the big painkiller freak-out a few years ago. Well, the one that started a few years ago. Still going on I guess. Anyway, the feds got kind of suspicious on account of her prescribing more narcotics than anyone else in the state many times over. Turns out the valedictorian is a bit of a Dr. Feelgood."

"Well, I don't suppose they could put her in here for that."

"They might have, but doesn't seem like they could really pin her down for any wrong doing. Doctors are slippery, you know. Pretty easy to wave around an X-ray and say that someone needs a certain pill. What's even more interesting is that even for a doctor, she had an all-star legal defense. Like miles beyond what a doctor could pay for… a whole team of lawyers from New York flew down. It went to hearing with the board, for the revocation of her license, but nothing happened."

Felix looked in the detective's eyes. *Let him do his mind reading now.*

"Listen. What you need to do young man, is take a chill pill of your own, if you will excuse the turn of phrase. I'm still investigating this Felix. I'm a professional detective. I've been doing this for years. Now it is time that you sit on the sidelines. If these people are what you think they are, then there is no sense in you sticking your neck out."

"How do I know they haven't gotten to you, too?" Felix said.

"Cause you'd be dead already," the old detective smirked. "But seriously. Young man, in such cases as this, there is nothing to do but follow your gut," he said.

Melancon walked over to within arm's length of Felix and stuck out his hand. It hurt, but Felix found himself grasping the detective's palm in a firm handshake.

"I can't promise I won't be involved," Felix said. "But I have to just trust you….don't I?"

"Yep. Now, I managed to get them to go with a standard bail amount on an aggravated assault charge, so you don't have to appear before a judge to get released. Your fiery Latin godfather is waiting outside with a blank check from your mother. So it looks like you are on your way out the door. Which is good because I've been sitting here for hours trying to prevent any funny business, and its past time for a drink. But you will have to appear in court later on Felix. Get your Mama's lawyers on it and you're probably looking at fines and community service in the worst case. But you will be found guilty. I mean, there were over 100 witnesses. It will probably go on your record."

"Yeah, it was pretty stupid wasn't it?"

Melancon laughed. "You're going to be alright kid. We're going to work this thing out."

Back in the lobby the woman at the counter looked Felix up and down. The benches were full and the floor squeaked with rubber soles.

Tomás was waiting. His face was heartbreaking.

The detective smiled when they got ready to say goodnight. "I'm going to go have a little talk with the Troxclairs. You two just keep your heads down until then, deal?"

"No promises. Anyway, it seems more likely they will come looking for us before we get the chance to do anything."

"Just don't go waving any more pistols around. It's Carnival time, after all. Have a beer kid."

After some paperwork, they drove home.

"I'm sorry Felix," Tomás said.

"For what?"

"I lost you in the crowd. This should not have happened."

"More like I should have stuck around you, Tomás. I about lost my mind chasing that float."

"What are you going to do next?"

"I just need a little time to think about it, I guess."

When they got inside, his mother was waiting for them.

"I'm going to be left with no sons at all," she said. When he didn't respond to this, she kept on.

"I've bailed you out of jail twice in one week Felix. I'd half expected you'd have some sort of speech prepared defending yourself."

"I'll be smarter next time."

She sipped her drink and looked at him.

"Why did you pull the gun out if you weren't going to use it son?" she asked.

"They got to me."

She looked at Tomás on the far side of the room. "What does he mean by that?"

"If you'll allow me, Madame…"

She nodded at him and Tomás went upstairs.

She turned back to her son. "You've lost your father's gun I assume?"

"Well they certainly didn't give it back to me at the police station."

"Here," she said, and reached into her purse. She pulled out a tiny black handgun and put it into Felix's open palm.

"Ruger 9 millimeter. I'm told it isn't very powerful, but I suppose you would be ill-advised to walk around with nothing after everything that has happened."

He welled up again, and put his arms around her. They were still embracing when Tomás landed at the bottom of the stairs with the plush train held out in front of him.

"What the hell is that?" She asked.

Chapter 17

Melancon figured there would be no trouble out at Spanish Turn. At least not of the immediate, life threatening kind. If there was one thing he knew about the rich, it was the gentle way they had of dodging their troubles. That wet-fish wriggling slipperiness of the moneyed was among the safest of bets, at least in his line of work. They'd smile and shake your hand and scratch their heads when questioned. "I'm not so sure about that, sir," or, "can't be certain on that account." Later you'd get a call from an overworked attorney. He'd experienced it plenty of times before.

So, he wasn't surprised at all when the gate sentry's attitude was chipper, expectant even, the way that mechanical arm shot right up. Of course he could come in. Didn't even have to show her his badge. She looked tired, stressed, and fat. Working for the rich was likely the same as investigating them. They would pat you on the back, tell you good job, and then later have the secretary draw up your pink slip. It was always hard to know where you stood with wealthy types.

Did they still even use pink slips? Probably not. He was probably just being dramatic, a tad bitter even that he himself had never been rich. Also, people he couldn't read made him uncomfortable.

It reminded him, being out here, of Evan Richards from high school. Evan had made a million in fried chicken joints and was now living somewhere out here in one of these regal houses. Melancon wouldn't dream of ever stopping by, but just being out here reminded him of another world, a place where even people he knew had occasionally flown off to.

He rolled his window down and smelled the air. These houses were obscene. The wind blew hard and on it was the smell of grass clippings and construction, a raw timber smell. Did you really need three stories on your house? And who were you trying to impress with those antebellum columns? The war was long over. And the yardmen were legion. He'd never seen so many in one place before.

But the neighborhood was dressed up for Carnival. They didn't miss an opportunity to showboat. Garish on top of garish, that much was sure, though maybe he'd stop short of saying the word *tacky*. There were streamers and banners and masks on porch railings. Tinsel wreaths and flags blowing in the breeze. The crepe myrtles were bare and everything else meticulously pruned. A sort of easy energy to it, the way that money had amplified it all, added many hands to the dress up, and made it all seem effortless.

But maybe he was thinking too much again. He did that. And he was no arbiter of taste, to be sure, but he felt the decorations might be lacking in heart. The whole neighborhood was ready for Carnival, and why wouldn't it be? They paid for their frivolity though. Perhaps it helped the rich to see their houses decked in gold and purple and a fleur de lis, helped them take their mind off their money for a while and remind themselves they could still be part of something universal and human. All they needed to do was sign a check or two.

His clothes were old, out of style. He wore suspenders and his fedora was tattered and oil smudged. Pulling into the Troxclair estate, Melancon found himself looking in the rearview mirror, straightening his tie, primping his blond tuft of remaining hair. He was worried about his appearance, his mild smell of tobacco from the cigars he chewed late at night, the plebian scarcity of his person. His home sported no grand decorations and there were no workers tending his lawn. He felt thin and old.

"What are you doing old man?" he asked himself, as he tried to properly part his tuft of hair and failed. "You're not out here to impress anybody. It's them that need to be worrying about their impression."

He knew what he was doing though. He was secretly worried that these people would think he was some kind of a drifter and shut the door in his face. It was an old fear, a class fear, a thing even Melancon with all his perception would have had trouble vocalizing, but knew in his gut.

These people could, possibly, in some set of crazy circumstances, actually *be killers*. Or more likely they were just people with a deadly will, worse maybe. The amplification of will was all around him. Money and power was what gave will its fangs.

But he likely had nothing to fear from the people themselves, he assured himself. It was one thing to put your hands around the neck of a fellow human, to slide a knife in their gut, or to pull the trigger against their skull; it was quite another to make a phone call, or to whisper in some dark hotel room. He'd be safe for now, but by years of habit he kept himself armed regardless.

He knocked, wondering if they'd pretend not to be in. Two Escalades rested in the driveway, one white one black.

Two of them, husband and wife, answered the door together. They smiled. He met their eyes, nodded. Were they waiting for him? Melancon got out his name, showed his badge. The lanky man was dressed in golfing clothes and instigated a fierce handshake, no hesitation or defensiveness about it. The woman was in a floral dress, though despite the unseasonable warmth she also wore a kind of shawl across her back. She fluttered her eyelashes at him. *What a face,* thought Melancon.

"And it is *Dr.* Lena Troxclair? No kidding?"

"Just call me Lena, you tall drink of water."

He felt himself being pulled into their gravity from the very start of the encounter. They invited him inside without asking a single question. They showed him artwork in their cavernous living room. A tribal mask of the something something tribe. Pictures of Safari in Kenya. Lena bowing to a sensei. Max dressed as a Lion some long ago Halloween. At some point in their cataloguing the wife handed him a drink. There were rules about that kind of thing, about drinking on the job, but Melancon wasn't one to pay too close attention to trivial rules that didn't suit him. His nerves had him sipping before his sense of professionalism could stop him.

Somewhere between the New York Marathon and a discussion of their niece, Melancon interjected.

"I've come to talk to you about quite an important matter," he said, helping himself to a seat on one of those high backed reading chairs he imagined had come from a headmaster's office somewhere.

The couple sat down in unison, set their drinks down on coasters in one fluid motion. Lena cocked her head. Max crossed his legs and put his hand to his chin. All at once they were somber, concerned, serious.

"I understand that you were recently elected as King and Queen of the…um." He pulled out his notepad. "Krewe of Ace-phalus."

"That's Asclepius," Lena said, letting the word roll off in her twangy way. Max nodded, cracking what Melancon felt was a boozy but cold smile.

"Can you tell me a little about your organization?"

She looked at him with wide, shimmering eyes. "Behold, I will bring to them health and healing, and I will heal them; and I will reveal to them an abundance of peace and truth."

"Ma'am?"

Max raised his eyes to his wife, who straightened her dress and beamed at him, then seemed to remember herself. "That is the motto. Of the krewe I mean. Of course. Well, let's see...right, it is thought to have started at the end of the civil war, when all the surgeons got back to town I suppose. I suppose... if you've sawed someone's leg off a few hundred times it might help to sort of have other's around who...I guess... had similar experiences. All men in those days of course. But even after the old sawbones died, their children, who were also doctors, took it up and turned it into a krewe. Now, in 1964 the city banned the krewe, due to some misunderstanding about the allocation of certain funds...among other little spats. But the krewe was kept alive. Every year they would start down on the bayou and march all the way up to the borders of Orleans Parish, where they would douse the torches and sadly disperse. A kind of protest, you know? But recently, the city and the Krewe have come to a new understanding. We've been members for years, you see, but only now have we sorted out those terrible past indiscretions. Just after medical school I joined. I had to talk Max into it of course, he isn't as gregarious as I am, you see."

"So, I guess the krewe has seen an uptick in membership, now that they've got their charter back?"

"Yes. It's always been sort of an…unofficial thing. Just doctors talking shop really. Nothing you'd find very interesting detective."

Melancon looked at the husband, and back to her. There was some electricity between them. He'd seen it, but had no idea what it meant. She certainly seemed nervous, flirtatious. It could be the badge that set her off, or it could be…

"What's this in regards to, anyway?" asked Max, cutting off the detective's train of thought.

Whatever it was, his gut was singing with inferences, perceptions, buzzing with feelings that he couldn't quite put a finger on. He was an old radio sifting through static for a signal.

"Well," Melancon started, "as I'm sure you know, a member of your krewe died under some mysterious circumstances last week."

"Robert," Lena said. She didn't seem to flinch from the name.

"Yes." Max looked from his wife to the detective, and then down at the floor. "He was a dear, dear friend."

Melancon raised his eyebrows. His face felt flush and twitchy. He decided to try and jar something loose from the woman.

Looking right at her: "Robert crawled under a train at night, down by the river, and let it slip over him. It chewed him into pieces. Nothing left really. Two kids. Wife. Practice. Even a little brother."

He watched their faces. Something. The woman's lips may have turned down a degree, her pupils may have fluttered a bit. Did her brow squeeze in concern? Shock? Offense? Violence? Melancon was having trouble concentrating. Something wasn't quite right.

"What information can we provide detective?" Max demanded in a new, harder voice. He was trying to draw Melancon's eyes towards him, the detective could see that clearly.

"Were you close to him?" Melancon asked.

A moment of uncertainty filled the room like molten lead.

"We respected each other," Max said, a bit too loudly. "I liked the man. Respected his character, and yes we spent a great deal of time together. Particularly lately. Planning and organizing mostly. But he was always just a little distant, Robert. Cold. We never spent real leisure time together. I thought he might have been sort of... aloof. I'm embarrassed to say, but, I had it in my mind that he considered my wife to be lower class than himself somehow, like maybe he thought her background might have made her less of a doctor or something. Even though I'm told Robert himself was brought up just as his family was rising. He was like that. A bit judgmental or imperious, prone to seeing flaws in others. It wouldn't surprise me one bit that he may have suffered from some form of depression. He never seemed...satisfied. But you know, I would have called him a friend, despite all that."

Melancon looked over at the wife.

"We were deeply saddened by the loss," she said.

"But you didn't go to the funerallll?"

Was he slurring his words? He shook his head and snapped out of it.

Lena looked at him, a sort of sadness in her eyes.

"A dear friend, yes, but under the circumstances we felt it best not to intrude on the family," she said, and rubbed her hands together, fretted, smacked her lips. Melancon noticed her hunchback for the first time then as she stood and walked over to the wall of pictures. How unfortunate, he thought, that such a beautiful woman should be shaped like some sort of sweet potato. That was what she looked like, really, a potato with the face of a knockout. Mrs. America Potato Head. He laughed out loud at the thought, to his own surprise, and shut his mouth as quick as he was able.

"So do you also know…do you know…about…" Melancon said, feeling a shakiness rise up in his chest. He put down the Sazerac immediately. It was very strong, and he feared he might have swallowed it more quickly than he realized. How early was it? Wasn't it before lunch? No breakfast down the hatch to even things out unfortunately. And suddenly he was very hungry for sweet potato.

Melancon felt embarrassed, but not that embarrassed. He had been a detective a long time, back when it was ok for a man to be a little drunk on the job before noon. But these were different times and…

"How do you feel detective," Lena said. "You look like you may be a bit ill."

I do feel a bit ill. But that face! Suddenly her hunchback don't seem so awful, and she has the most darling face I've ever seen, like she's straight out of an old black and white picture.

He realized then that he had been saying it all out loud, that the already frail filter between his thoughts and speech had completely dissolved.

"We aren't bad, detective," Max was saying, suddenly transported to the side of the chair with his hand on Melancon's shoulder.

"We are good people," the gorgeous face said, now standing over him like an angel.

Next thing he knew she was leading him upstairs. It was the oddest thing, because even though he felt horrified at the thought of going upstairs in this cavernous mansion, he found his feet plodding heavily one after the other, skyward. His mind seemed a thing separate from him.

Was he dead? Had he died? He was so sleepy but these people were not so bad. Perhaps they were trustworthy.

Max has a firm handshake, looks like he would be a good boxer too. A real man's man. The kind of guy who makes strong Sazeracs and drinks them for brunch without a second thought. He can handle his liquor. Real strong jaw, looks like it could take a punch.

"Detective," someone, someplace was saying. "We are so glad you could stop by for a social visit. We'll have to play a round of golf sometime soon. Sleep well."

And then the world went black.

Chapter 18

Melancon woke up in a strange bed. He didn't know the time, had left his old flip phone out in the car. There was still some daylight outside, but with long shadows and an orange tint to the beams streaming in the windows.

"Hello?" he called out. A loud echo came back at him.

"Detective?" Footsteps, a woman's, clacking up the wooden stairs.

"Mrs. Troxclair?"

She appeared in the threshold.

"Your old men shall dream dreams, and your young men shall see visions," she said over him, sounding pleased about it.

His coat hung from one of the bed posts, and he pawed at it, rifling through the pockets. He wanted his notepad. When he managed to fish it out, he read the last words he had written on its pages: "no motive, no evidence, no case," in big blocky letters. His gun belt was draped on the floor.

Melancon was sixty-two years old, just getting accustomed to the many weaknesses that came with advancing age, but he'd certainly never dealt with anything like this before— with falling asleep in the middle of the day while working.

"I'm sorry…" was all he could think to say.

"Not at all detective. In fact, I've seen this sort of thing happen a lot in some of my patients. Usual cause is a sudden drop in blood sugar. That can be brought on by stress, you know. A man your age ought to be taking it a little easier. Have you made plans for your retirement?"

He rubbed his eyes, as much in disbelief as sleepiness, and tested his legs before he stood up.

"No. I…I don't know what came over me."

Embarrassed he added: "Just…call me if you remember anything about Robert. Anything you think I should know about."

The husband remained unseen. Lena stood in the doorway watching him collect himself, her hands clasped together at her stomach. She nodded, glowed like a waxing moon.

"It is such a shame that you'd come all the way out here and waste your time. But then I guess you caught up on your sleep anyway."

After rubbing the blur from his eyes the beautiful face and the unfortunate haunch behind it had now become quite clear and lucid.

"I'm embarrassed."

"Don't be detective. No one down at the station ever has to know a thing about this. I *do* have some friends down at the precinct, but I don't see that this as even worth mentioning to them. No, certainly not. You simply had a senior moment. Nothing to get too worked up about. And no one *has to* know, as I said. Let's just put this whole thing behind us and move on with our lives. What do you say to that detective?"

She walked him to the door, pulling at his sleeves, shaking her head at him as he tried to speak.

At the threshold, they stood facing each other.

"I suppose you'll be making the rounds to all of Roberts's friends and acquaintances?" She asked.

"We'll see."

She looked at him down her nose now, and a tightness came into her face.

"I hope no one has been filling your head with gossip about us detective."

He squinted his eyes at her. "I may call on you again. The investigation is still ongoing."

"Do not give the devil a foothold," she said, shading her eyes from the long rays of the sunset.

He gave her one last look over. There was certainly something about her. Some granite-like quality. As if she and that hillock on her shoulders had always been, always would be. She wore her feminine charm like a costume, but he could see right through it, even in his daze. Her eyes gave it away. Deep down she was hard, sure of herself, driving towards something. But what?

With a nod of the head, she closed the door on him.

Back in his car, the real uncertainty seeped in. Had he really fallen asleep during the middle of an interrogation? Had his blood sugar spiked and if so, should he take a day or two off? What was it about these two that had unsteadied him in the first place? Had he been ridiculous to drive out to this gilded bit of swamp to ask questions of two doctors based on the hunches of some kid? He really hadn't learned anything specific. But his gut was shouting something, albeit in a language foreign to him.

The engine on his old El Camino cranked right up and he sped out of the front gate of the subdivision. The sun was setting now over the marshes and it was as if you could hear the snakes and mosquitos bubbling up out of the living water. Melancon lowered his window and, deciding that the fresh air could do him some good, leaned his head out, with his hat steadied by his left hand.

That was when he saw the black Plymouth, coming along behind.

It floated in the side mirror, a silent creature out of the swamp confirming that nagging feeling still stirring beneath all the muddiness of his senses. Something wasn't right here. It wasn't only the Plymouth, but everything: the whole world had gone off kilter, taken a wrong turn someplace back a while ago. Whatever sixth sense the detective possessed, it cramped with inferences, with a niggling uncertainty, substantiated in the reflection of that black vehicle. It was the only car on the road, and behind it the sun was just now setting over the marsh.

Melancon rolled his window up slowly, turning the old manual crank to raise the glass. He was awake enough now. His fingers wandered down to the cool metal of his revolver. They ran along the crosshatched hammer. It hadn't been pulled out in anger in some time, he thought, years maybe. He found himself attempting to pull it out now, fussing with the small leather holster. He ended up having to unbutton it with his front teeth, steering wheel in one hand. As he did he hit a pothole, and that caused the gun to slip out and fall between the seats.

"Goddamn it. Pull it together old man."

Maybe he *was* getting old, but he had the sinking suspicion that if he didn't fish that gun out in a hurry, he wouldn't be getting too much older. Once he had it he placed it on the passenger seat. Next, he pulled out something from his glove box. It was a small electronic device, a GPS tracker. Then, without indicating, Melancon threw his rusty El Camino onto the ample shoulder of LA-406. He reached down and snapped up the pistol and the device in one quick motion and stepped out to meet his fate.

But he wasn't waiting to see what this was all about. The day had been unsettling enough, the sun was falling in the west, blinding him, and the swamp was unknowable. His usefulness and power were moribund. He was old and he didn't wait for things any longer. He stood in the middle of the highway, his pistol pointed forward, ready to jump off into the swamp if the Plymouth didn't stop.

It was the fourth or fifth time he'd seen this car on his tail, always imagining it to be a coincidence. But his talk with Felix had convinced him otherwise. Even so, his last thought before the Plymouth pulled over was that maybe he had made some kind of mistake. The car would pull over and it would be some soccer mom from Spanish Turn absolutely shitting her pants and already calling her lawyer shouting, "SUE, SUE, SUE."

But it pulled over and sat with its engine idling. If the occupants were frightened, combative, or litigious, they gave no indication behind the tinted windshield.

"Out of the car!" screamed Melancon. He had to be scary now, to have his hackles up.

The window rolled down, a voice inside said, "What you going to do with dat, old man?"

It was a voice Melancon instantly recognized.

"Earl," the detective said.

It was the puckered face cop who had brought in Felix that first night. Melancon walked over cautiously.

"Where is your lackey?" Melancon asked. He'd lowered his piece but was still gripping the sturdy metal.

"I'm right here you old fuck, but I ain't no man's lacky," Smith croaked from the passenger seat.

"What the hell are you two wound up into? Why have you been following me?"

"Aw get over yourself detective," Smith let out, his arms crossed in front of his chest.

"We are just kinda....moonlighting I guess you could say," Earl said with a jagged smile.

They seemed tense. The sky was growing darker.

"Who are you working for?"

"Personal security for an undisclosed client," Earl said.

"Is that a fact? Are they paying you to follow me around? To harass Felix Herbert?"

They went stony after that, faces forward, jaws clenched. The air conditioner buzzed and the engine whirred. Earl put his hands back on the wheel.

"If you are going to arrest us, you need a warrant."

"Probable cause is good enough for me."

"Go ahead and try it Dick Tracy," Earl said, and his fingers gave a slight flutter. It was then that the detective noticed Earl's service pistol sitting plainly on the dashboard, not a foot from where his hands rested on the steering wheel. Earl saw the detective see the gun, and they looked at each other.

Melancon went into that place. It was a place he'd gone many times before, somewhere he couldn't conjure up or even describe if hard pressed. The place an animal goes.

He peered deep into Earl's wet pebble eyes and found he could read the text of them there, quite clearly.

It was something simple there, something binary. There was to be no talking to this scowl faced man and his burly partner. These two were unafraid and determined as only a rigid stupidity could allow.

He looked at the gun, he looked at Earl.

"I know what is going on here," Melancon said. "And I also know that if I try to arrest you, you will shoot me. Or maybe you are planning on shooting me anyway. Now. It might be possible that I shoot both of you in the head within a perfectly timed second or two, and you'd never get the chance to return fire. But none of these options seem really appealing. Now, I know and you know that Earl and Smith are not smart men, but you are smart enough to know that none of the things I described need to happen. You are smart enough men to just drive away now."

They said nothing, but their faces could hold no lies.

"Alright," Melancon said. "I'm going to set my pistol down here in the grass. And I'm going to stay bent down like that until you two drive away. And I don't want to see you following me anywhere else. But if I so much as hear that car door crack open, I'm coming up shooting. You've got my word on that."

"You're going senile Detective," Earl said.

"Ok then, slowly now." Melancon bent down but he did not put the gun in the grass. As his right trouser leg soaked in the swamp water, he used his free had to stick the tracking device just under the front tire well with a quick two fingers.

He waited a moment. When a minute passed and they hadn't moved he stood back up and faced them. Their eyes were cold, watchful, and tired. They looked away from him and at each other. Then they looked at the pistol in his hand, dangling now from his side. A nod.

In that tense moment an electric cackle sparked to life inside the cab.

"Car 72, car 72, be advised....." and then only static. Three long seconds of it in which Melancon felt the radiated waves of hope bouncing around his insides.

"This is dispatch, we are looking for Officer Smith. What is your location?" the voice said.

They continued to watch the detective. No one moved. The radio kept going.

"We've got a 10-55 over here on Claiborne. State trooper pulled the guy over. They are wondering where the local responding officer is. I told them that was you."

Smith's eyes sank.

"The GPS is showing the location on your squad car as being parked in a shopping mall on the West Bank, what the hell are you doing over there?"

Finally, he picked up the receiver. "This is Smith. I'm responding now. Just had a personal situation to deal with. Let's keep it between us alright Gina. I'm taking my kid to the doctor."

"You better get over here Smith. I won't say anything but you know this trooper will if you don't show up quick."

"Ten four."

Both officers faced forward for a moment. Earl turned and let his pebble eyes rest on Melancon's.

The tinted window slid up and over them and the detective could see no more. The sun was down. A coyote howled. The tires squealed and Melancon was soon watching the red tail lights fall in with the dusk.

His heart was beating in his throat and he stood around a moment letting it settle. Then he drove. The moon came out from behind a cloud and there was an owl that passed in front of his headlights as he rolled down the highway. There he was in his own rear view mirror, the wrinkled brow and white bushy eyebrows. He'd lived this long on instinct.

He increased his speed. Locked the door to his small cottage on West Napoleon. Poured himself three fingers of scotch. After the booze loosened him he checked his pistol, the hunch growing more insistent with each bitter sip.

All six bullets had been removed by someone, the chambers empty and eternal in the kitchen light.

That night he would dream terrible, horrible things. He'd wake up after seeing himself riddled with holes, drifting along in the swamp. In the dream, nutria rats used his corpse as a buoyant little island, hornets feasted on his eyeballs, and the white of his skin went scaly and green as he moldered down into the vast, black water of forever.

Chapter 19

Mrs. Herbert studied the train for some time. She sat in the parlor, turning the little locomotive engine in her papery hands and squeezing the plush thoughtfully. Ten minutes passed, until she finally put it down on the table as Tomás set a tray of coffee out for them. The fire had turned to embers now, and Felix's father sat near the coals with his gray head drooping down onto his chest. Outside the city crews were scraping the Avenue clean from the latest parade, and the sound of shovels against asphalt rang through the house.

"Scopodol…" she said.

Both Felix and Tomás watched her closely now.

"Scopodol…" she repeated, stirring her coffee with a spoon.

"Tomás," she finally said. "Would you be a doll and go up to the master bathroom, look behind the mirror on the left. Second, or maybe top shelf. There should be a few prescription bottles there. Bring me what you find."

"Certainly Madame."

She looked over to her son. "That is, if you haven't pilfered them all by now."

Felix reddened.

"Actually, I've been on the wagon."

"Is that so?"

"Yes, I haven't had any drugs since shortly after Robert's death." He paused, looking at her. "Aren't you proud of me?"

"For he on honey-dew hath fed! And drunk the milk of Paradise!" His father spurted from his corner.

"Yes, Felix. I'm proud," she said.

Felix's redness deepened. He turned to his father. "You'd be proud too dad, wouldn't you?"

The old man rocked in his seat. "If you tell the truth, you don't have to remember anything," he mumbled.

"That's right dear," Mrs. Herbert said. "Our son here was just telling me that he has overcome his drug addiction. It's quite good news."

"Quite good, quite good," the old man said, and drooped again.

"I'm not sure how well you remember the time just after your father's breakdown?"

Of course he remembered. His sophomore year at Tulane. The doctors, Robert included, had said it was a stroke, but

Felix knew it had been something deeper, some subterranean pressure that had been building for years and had finally erupted.

"You remember how he was, just after?"

As Felix sat there thinking, remembering, Tomás came down the stairs with an armful of pill bottles. It was, indeed, the same selection from which Felix had been accustomed to pilfering.

Tomás unloaded his arms on the ottoman and stood back looking at the dozen or so tubes of orange plastic. Mrs. Herbert leaned over the pile and one by one stacked them on the table, until one of the bottles in particular gave her pause.

"Here it is."

And she tossed it to Felix.

"Scopodol – take 2 tablets every 4-6 hours as needed for restlessness, anxiety, pain and insomnia.

"Quite the panacea," Tomás whispered.

Who gave you these Mom?"

"It was Dr. Capdeau. Maybe. Your father took them for a while, but then he stopped because…"

She seemed to sink deep in thought for a moment. She walked over to Felix and took the bottle, shaking it a bit in her outstretched hand.

"Because…your brother…"

She stared at the bottle. "Your brother wouldn't ever just be our doctor," she finally said. "He claimed it would make his judgement cloudy to treat his own parents, that there were things best left to the discretion of a third party. That always disappointed me."

Felix reached out for the drug. "But he still kept an eye on your medications, didn't he. I remember him doing the same with me."

"Yes. He'd always check in after the fact and we'd talk about what the doctor had said. A second opinion, something like that."

"What did Robert think about this Scopodol?" Tomás asked from the wall.

"I don't believe he approved...yes. He advised us not to let your father take it. He said that there was something wrong with it, that it needed further testing...oh I don't remember precisely, but I definitely recall that he wasn't very happy with Dr. Capdeau....not at all. But I can't remember if anything ever came of it. I just put them in the cabinet and forgot about them."

Felix could feel his blood rising.

"I saw the drug in *her* drawer in Spanish Turn. Now it appears on the Mardi Gras throws? We know Robert didn't like it."

Tomás uncrossed his arms and stepped forward. "Felix! That could mean..."

"We don't know anything for certain old friend. But it certainly is a lot of coincidences."

Mrs. Herbert rested a hand on her chin. "What do you think husband?"

The old man was silent, watching her but saying nothing.

"Let's just say this Scopodol does have to do with what is going on," Felix began. "If these little pills have something to do with it, I need to know exactly what they do. Obviously, they don't just cause you to drop dead the second you eat them. If it was a matter of poisoning by drug, Robert's autopsy would have shown any overdose, right? And you said Dad took them for a while to calm down a bit. And he is still here, after all. So there must be something else. Maybe it is something…behavioral."

Felix dumped a pill out into his palm.

"What are you doing?" Tomás gasped.

Felix looked from the pill to his old friend's knowing eyes.

"You shall not!"

"Why not? I need to figure out how they might affect a person, and better to do it now in a safe place than have it sneak up on me later."

"You're not going to Felix. You are finished with all that."

"But this is for Robert," Felix said.

It happened too fast, before he could react. As Felix cast his eyes about for his cup of coffee to swallow the tablet down, Tomás snatched it out of his hand, put it in his own mouth, and swallowed it dry.

They all stared at him, even Mr. Herbert, who croaked: "And all should cry beware! Beware! His flashing eyes, his floating hair!"

There was an uneasy smile on Felix's face while ten tense minutes passed. Not much was said. Still Tomás was insisting he felt fine.

Then, the doorbell broke the silence.

"I'll see who it is," Tomás declared, and before they could stop him, he'd left the room. They all listened. When it rang again, Felix stood up and walked to the foyer, where he found Tomás peering at the security screen and not moving.

"Well who is it?"

But before the old man could respond, the taciturn security guard had opened the front door and stuck his head in. "Are you expecting anyone?" he asked.

Felix gazed into the monitor. Its camera showed the gate that led to the front path and up to their steps. There, in the grainy feed of the CCTV, was Melancon's face looking tired and inflated by the lens.

"Yes, he is a friend. You can let him in."

Like hope itself, Melancon was slow on his feet, shuffling his way into the foyer wearing a stained shirt and awfully out-of-date suspenders.

"I'm starting to believe you Felix," the detective said.

"You have been out?" Tomás asked heavily.

"Well I was able to go talk to them, to the Troxclairs."

179

"And? Out with it man!" Tomás was far from relaxed, Felix noted.

"Something about the whole experience of going out there... I don't know, it was weird."

"Weird?" Felix said.

Melancon took off his hat and reached into his shirt pocket for his cigar, clearly forgetting that it wasn't there. He seemed lost, dazed, confused about why he had come. It wasn't the usual sharp-witted, fast-talking detective that Felix had been starting to warm to. This was a senior, going gray, forgetting just where he'd parked the car.

Felix's eyebrows went up. "Do you mean that they were weird people, or that they behaved strangely, or that something in the environment was off-putting? What?"

"For once, I'm at a loss for words kid. Say, can I get a cup of coffee or something? I need to collect my thoughts."

They all sat down in the parlor. Melancon nodded to Mrs. Herbert.

"Ma'am," he said, and helped himself to the coffee on the table.

They all leaned back. No one looked at each other. Coffee was sipped. Each head seemed to be swimming with its own thoughts, until Felix felt a jolt of frustration.

"You said they were weird?" he insisted, putting down his cup and leaning forward at Melancon.

The detective let out a long sigh and nodded his head, looking now from the bottle of pills to the little plush train on the table, and back again.

Tomás guffawed. "Well this is all very *weird*, detective. This is not helpful information….we…."

Tomás looked like he would say more, and opened his mouth again, but no words came out. They all turned their heads to him, expectant and then confused. A look of fear flashed over his dark face then, and his head bobbed three times. On the last bob he slumped. It drew a gasp from Mrs. Herbert, and Felix was up before he had time to think, catching the old man's trembling shoulder and helping him lay back.

Melancon had jolted up as well, and leaned over Tomás. The detective produced a small flashlight from his pocket and shone it in the old man's eyes, the pupils of which were gaping.

"What's wrong with him?" Melancon asked.

Felix, after making sure his friend was in a safe position, reached over to the table and tossed the little plush train at Melancon. "He tested a drug on himself. *The drug*. The same drug advertised on the train they threw at me. The same one I found in their house. And the same one my brother seemed to disapprove of."

"Scopodol. You just happened to have some lying around huh?"

"It was for my husband's condition. What do you know about it detective?" Felix's mother asked.

Melancon circled the couch, keeping his eyes on Tomás where he lay.

"It feels very familiar, I'll tell you that."

Tomás' forehead shone with sweat and his breath was heavy. Felix sat down next to him and fretted. "Are you still with us?" he asked, patting his friend's face gently.

Tomás grinned, his eyes lolling loose in their sockets.

"How do you feel old man?"

"I guess I am feeling... old," Tomás laughed to himself.

"Do you feel sort of, drunk? Dizzy? Like you might fall asleep?" The detective asked.

"I've never been drunk before," Tomás replied, trying to sit up but being restrained.

Felix and the detective looked at each other with puzzled expressions.

"Well, do you feel bad?" Felix asked.

Tomás looked down at his body and palmed himself a few times. He appeared to be finding it all funny.

"No, I feel fantastic... just too tired."

The detective crouched down, eye level with Tomás.

"I think he is going to be fine."

Felix backed up a few feet, feeling the shakiness in his knees. It had scared the hell out of him.

"I think we should try something," Melancon said, glancing over his shoulder at Felix.

"What...on Tomás? He's not a goddamn guinea pig."

Melancon shrugged and turned back towards Tomás on the couch.

"What if I told you to punch your young friend here in the face?" the detective said, addressing the writhing old man.

Felix furrowed his brow. "What?"

The detective gave out a tight chuckle. "Just indulge me here a second, son. Don't worry, you're not made of glass."

Tomás wore a little disgusted expression on his face. But he didn't seem to object very strongly to the suggestion. They all watched him for a moment until Mrs. Herbert began to read from her cellphone.

"I found some information on a message board. Drug information for Scopodol, made by Halcyon Pharms. Let's see.... Do you feel light headed?"

Tomás nodded.

"Is the experience almost unreal? Like a dream? Does it strike you as less concrete than normal? Do you find yourself doubting what is happening?"

"How is he going to answer all that mom," Felix said. "Can't you see the poor guy is exhausted?"

The old man's eyes widened for a moment and then closed. They all continued to monitor him until it became clear that he had simply fallen asleep. He now looked to be perfectly peaceful, and his breathing had evened out and his lips moved with inaudible Spanish nothings.

Melancon took another sip at the coffee. "I don't know. I don't have any experience with drugs. Well, not since the sixties anyway. The last thing I remember I was asking them questions…and then…"

Felix's mind had been too focused on his friend, but now it did an about face and realized the significance of what the detective was saying.

"You mean…You started feeling a bit funny?" Felix said.

The detective nodded over his mug. "They had served me a Sazerac as well. Which I lapped up, damned old fool that I am."

Felix looked directly into the detective's eyes. "These people are doing something with this drug, something bad."

Melancon put down his coffee and held the plush train up to his face for closer inspection.

"We still need a lot of things kid. A motive. Evidence of wrong doing. You know…we need a case," he said.

"You're the detective, right?"

"What are we going to do son? Bring a plush train into a court of law and submit it as exhibit A? Show them a video tape of your butler acting goofy? We have to get some kind of solid evidence here. Think about how these things really work. Your feeling that there is some drug-fueled cabal throwing people under trains and then taunting their relatives— it might mean something to you, but a bunch of talk about pills and trains isn't going to mean shit to a jury."

"So what do you suggest we do?"

"I think for starters I need to do a little snooping around on this drug of yours. Find out what we can about people who took it, are taking it. What is the status with the DEA? What does the FDA think about this? Why is it prescribed and at what rate? Now, I don't know how all of that is going to incriminate the Troxclairs. We need proof that they are doing something clearly illegal. A doctor writing prescriptions for a legal drug is not usually anything to investigate, but like I've told you before, our lady has a history of overprescribing particularly addictive drugs. The DEA absolutely hates that. So it might just give us a starting point if we can find out that she is doing the same here."

"She has bottles and bottles of pills in her desk, more than you could imagine. And they put up a fucking remote camera in one of the trees in our back yard. Scared my mother half to death."

The detective looked up from his coffee. Mrs. Herbert was watching him closely.

"Ma'am," he said respectfully, "I'll take that camera and check it for fingerprints, though if these people are the way your son is claiming they are, the chances of finding usable prints will be slim. I can also have our tech people check if there might be a way to find where the signal is…was… going. I don't know much about that kind of tech, but I've got some smart people that definitely do."

Tomás had woken up and was smiling out at them all.

"You are all very fine people," he said, as if to himself.

"You aren't so bad yourself, Tomás."

Detective Melancon stood up and brushed himself off. "I'm going to take care of this, you just have to be patient."

"I wish I could," Felix said, handing him the little camera.

"Don't do anything dumb, I mean, don't do anything else dumb."

"Having family murdered makes people do dumb things."

"Waving guns around at doctors is going to land you in Angola, and that's not a place you can win this battle from." The detective drained his coffee, grabbed up one of the tiny napkins from the tray, touched it to his head in the direction of Felix's mother, as if it were some kind of salute. He tipped his hat with the other hand and began moving towards the front door of the Herbert mansion.

Over his shoulder: "Just let me do a bit of poking around kid. It's what I do. Walk me out?"

On the front steps, the detective turned back to Felix.

"Look, I didn't want to say anything in front of your mother back there, but listen closely. If you see those two beat cops, that Smith and Earl again, do me one favor."

"Yeah?"

"Run."

Felix nodded.

"And if you can't run, tell them Melancon knows what they are up to, and he's going to take them to account for every dirty move they make."

They shook on it.

When Felix walked back into the parlor, Tomás stood and punched him square in the face.

Chapter 20

Felix watched closely as Tomás buttered the toast, spooned sugar onto the grapefruit, poured the coffee. No step missed. A perfect breakfast. He'd even remembered the special Carnival salt and pepper shakers.

"Sleep well, old man?"

Tomás bowed his head. "Very well sir. I slept like the dead— but I did have some odd dreams."

What those dreams were, he didn't share. Nor did he seem particularly disturbed by anything at all that morning. His movements were graceful, his voice sharp and clear, the uniform he wore as pressed as ever. After they'd begun to eat, Tomás went to fetch the man of the house. He pushed Felix's father into the room, placed the old pork baron in his perpetual corner and set his grits and ham on the tray before him.

Mrs. Herbert chewed the toast thoughtfully. "You gave quite a performance last night."

Tomás raised an eyebrow. "Did I, Madame?"

"You really have no memory of it?" Felix asked, putting down his fork.

"Of what, sir?"

"Tell me what you think happened last night."

The old man straightened himself, glancing out the window. "The grass will need to be mowed soon I'm afraid. I'll phone the lawn service. Bloody warm for a February now."

Felix tapped his fingers impatiently on the dining room table. "Tomás you punched me in the face. Don't you remember? Taking the Scopodol? Seeing Melancon? Any of it?"

Tomás went bug eyed. "I did what?"

Mrs. Herbert was chuckling, hiding her laugh behind the half-eaten slice of rye bread.

"Incredible. You honestly don't remember." Felix slapped some marmalade on his toast and thought about it.

"Remember what, sir?"

"I can see it in your face that you are surprised. But set your mind at ease on that account. You've done more for me than I could have asked for. You may have brought another clue to light here. Last night you were essentially a blank slate for three hours."

"TABULA RASA," his father sputtered from his corner, grits running down his chin. Tomás tutted to himself and grabbed up a napkin from the table.

"You punched me, seemingly on a suggestion that Melancon had made about ten minutes prior. Mom gasped and dropped her cup of coffee on the floor. It was a soft punch, grazing, without any emotion or passion in it. I was not hurt, but I was definitely shocked."

Tomás, for his part, looked as if he might cry hearing all this.

"And then you fell asleep, didn't you wonder when you woke up on the couch?"

"I did think it strange…"

"Devoid of any will whatsoever," Felix continued across the room. "And now, with a bit of sleep, you are completely returned to your old self, and you can't even remember what it was that you did."

Tomás returned and sat down with them at the table, laying down the grit smeared napkin. He looked at Mrs. Herbert in disbelief. "Is this all true?"

She nodded at him.

"Why Felix, I'm terribly terribly…"

"No Tomás, none of that. I'm fine really. It was for the sake of figuring out what we are up against, and you've done a great experiment. Shed some light on this thing. I mean, if this Scopodol really does make you as suggestable as it seems to do, then…well, it isn't out of the realm of possibility that it could be used for nefarious purposes. That it could be used to convince someone to do something…not in their best interest?"

"Such as..." Tomás lowered his brow. They wouldn't say it, not in front of Mrs. Herbert.

"Yes, Tomás."

She cleared her throat from across the table, patted her lips with a napkin, and said, "You mentioned something about a plan last night son. I don't know what you may have in mind, but I can't imagine it is going to improve our situation. So I do hope you've abandoned it."

"My plan, Mother, is just to go to Lena's clinic. I found it on a mapping program last night. Would you believe it's inside a strip mall out in Metairie?"

"Why would that be out of the ordinary?"

"Well, I suppose I just pictured it being a bit more imposing than that. I mean, it shares a wall with the damn Piccadilly."

"And what do you intend to do once there?"

Just then, the dark suited man who watched over them stuck his head into the dining room where they all sat. He nodded to the table.

"All is quiet ma'am," he said. "I'm going to walk the block and take a look around."

"Thank you," his mother replied.

"Wait a second. Greg, isn't it?" Felix stood and walked towards him.

"Yes sir, Greg."

"Greg." Felix paused, wanting to say it the right way. A robin landed just outside the dining room window and blustered at its own reflection.

"I wonder what your policy is on loaning equipment."

"Sir?"

"I know you have some surveillance equipment out there in the van, right? Cameras. Recording devices. 'Bugs' and so forth— if that is what you still call them. So, I'm eating my breakfast and I'm wondering: might there be any way you could use one of those listening devices to hear what was being said on the other side of a wall?"

Greg glanced around the room at all of them. He seemed to be considering what to say next.

"Of course. That is pretty basic technology sir. Not much more than a stethoscope with a few microphones attached... and a battery."

"Well, say I wanted to borrow one of those from you for the day."

His mother put down her teacup, shook her head, and got up from the table.

Greg looked stricken. "Sir?"

"I'd bring it back, of course. And no one has to know about it."

Greg looked behind himself, back out at the driveway, in the direction of the van and its beguiling "Valois Lawn Care Service" lettering.

"That would be a breach of protocol. I don't own the equipment. The firm does."

"Once more, into the breach dear friends, once more!" Mr. Herbert gurgled, and then fell asleep.

But Felix pretended not to notice. "It would be just for an hour or two."

Greg shook his head. "I can't do it young man. It isn't my equipment to lend."

"Two thousand dollars."

"I…"

"Three thousand? How about we make it an even five."

"Sorry sir. I've got my code. Just like I'm sure you have yours. We just don't lend out this stuff to civilians. What do you want it for anyway?"

"That's beside the point. You are telling me that there is no way I can convince you to lend us the equipment, is that what you are telling me?"

"That's right sir."

Felix let his shoulders go limp and sat back down. Tomás was watching him closely. The bottle of Scopodol sat in the middle of the table, right next to the pitcher of orange juice. Felix looked at it, and then at Tomás. The light of understanding lit up in the old man's eyes. He was still a sharp one.

The butler stood, brushed off the table cloth, and turned to Greg.

"Very good sir, may I offer you a drink before you make your excursion?"

Chapter 21

It wasn't lost on Felix that he'd done a bad thing, a thing of the very sort that the people he was hunting might have done. He told himself that omelets had to be made, something about desperate times, and a host of other excuses, but still he felt bad about it. He felt awful, in fact, but not nearly so guilty as worried. Worried that he'd left his mother alone with Greg: a man, at least temporarily, unable to render any assistance should the worst happen.

"It was only half a pill," Tomás was saying, as he piloted the Continental down Veterans Boulevard, out to the suburb of Metairie. "Half a pill and he coughed up everything we wanted."

"Powerful stuff. Seems kind of dangerous to have a drug like that lying around the house," Felix said. "Would be more fitting at some kind of interrogation camp somewhere."

In the backseat two listening devices, a recording device, and a camera with a large telescopic lens rattled softly against each other, all in a black leather bag. They had just grabbed the things most resembling the images Felix had looked up on the internet.

"I'm sure we could have gotten him to spit out some juicy secrets as well," Tomás smiled.

"He looked a little young to know where the bodies are buried, Tomás. Regardless, let's just hope it wears off before anything bad happens back at the home place. Let's talk about what our plan is."

They slowed to a crawl in a school zone near a wide canal. The black water was dull looking, and there was a fog. Ugly mottled geese nestled on the banks.

"Ah yes, this plan of yours."

"I've always loved Piccadilly. We simply go in, find a booth near where we think Lena's office might be, and sit drinking sweet tea and listening. We're bound to hear something at some point. Something worth bringing to Melancon."

Tomás tapped the steering wheel. A kid dropped his backpack near the curb and the crossing guard raised his stop sign.

"So. You don't trust Melancon to do this Felix?"

"He is sharp enough Tomás, but fuck waiting. I've been waiting my whole life. If Robert were here and I was dead and gone, I know he wouldn't wait one second."

"You're right about that my boy."

They arrived. He and Tomás sat for a long while in the lot, doing what they imagined detectives must be doing when they talked about "casing" a place in old movies. They had been at it for at least an hour and seen absolutely nothing of interest. There was no armed guard, no lines around the block, no fancy cars except for a white escalade parked in the handicap spot up front.

"I'm not sure what I expected," he said to Tomás, and turned up the air conditioning.

A "For Lease" sign hung in what looked like an old Blockbuster, the blue marquee all faded. The parking lot was full of smokers, workers from the cell phone store at one end, which seemed to be the only place with many customers. It was more pathetic than threatening. They eyed the Piccadilly.

"Worked up an appetite yet, old man?"

The cafeteria was dimly lit, and full of the very old. Steam rose up over the sneeze guard and he ordered the chopped beef, Tomás the catfish. But when they sat down they both found themselves not hungry.

The booth they had chosen was towards the back of the building, a room which had clearly once been a smoking section before such things were outlawed. The walls were yellowing and the plush of the booth smelled of tar. But, if they had calculated correctly, this would be the right spot. The wall they sat next to was definitely shared by the clinic. By the back of the clinic, more specifically, where the doctor's consultation rooms tend to be located. Tomás set the black bag on the plush next to him, and they waited while the hostess introduced herself, got their drinks, and made her mark on the ticket.

Felix scanned what sections of the dining room he could still see through the lattice. It was perfect really: the low light, the isolation of the smoking room, and no one but a few seniors nodding over their mashed potatoes and gumming their okra. Now, if they could only get a clear sound from the other side of that wall, if only they had a secret window into her office, they could begin to do *something*.

It took another hour. They sipped sweet tea and tried to appear as if they weren't waiting on a thing. Twice the hostess appeared and asked if they needed anything, but Tomás had thrown his jacket over the listening equipment. Both had the Bluetooth buds tucked discreetly into their ears.

And then they heard it. It began with an intense shuffling of papers, a bit of static, and the squeaking of rubber soles on that linoleum so ubiquitous in clinics. But the noise dissipated, until at last a clear female voice rang out. It was distinctly Lena Troxclair's.

"You're late," she said.

A man's voice, deep and slow, answered her.

"I'm not a delivery boy Lena. If you are in such a hurry, you know where our office is located."

"I'm a doctor…"

The voices faded in and out on the listening device now. It sounded as if Lena had turned to face away from the wall.

"Stay here and listen Felix, I'll take the other device to the next table and see what I can hear." Tomás stood up, the tangled web of batteries and wires hung in his arms.

It was then that the hostess poked her head in the smoking room. She looked at him and he froze. Tomás stood there with the wires dangling from his arms and put on an insincere smile. She was an old woman with cigarette lips and a grey ponytail. Her eyes went down to the devices, and back up to his face. She turned and went the other direction.

"We have to be quick now Felix."

He soon had the listening device connected to the wall again, and now the sounds of the office were coming through crystal clear. He waved Felix over and clicked the red button marked "record" on the device, hoping it would work as intended.

"So how many this week?" the man was asking.

"Two dozen at least, will have to double check the records. We might need to rotate out for another product though. Some people are starting to complain about memory loss and stuff."

"Well, let's just hope they forget to complain, shall we?"

"You've got the money, so I suppose you make the rules. Speaking of?"

"Yes, just like we agreed. But we really need to start doing this downtown. I don't think a Metairie strip mall is quite the right place for..."

Felix could hear the rolling wheels of the doctor's stool. "That's all of it?" Lena said.

"Yup, that is ten."

They looked at each other then, Tomás and Felix, over the wooden booth divider, and smiled.

"I think we've got something sir," Tomás said.

"The nail in the coffin would be to go out into the parking lot and snap a photo of this suit and maybe his license plate. Think we could do that discreetly?"

"You can do anything Felix, I'm convinced."

They waited for the conversation to end. They then threw the equipment back in the bag, tangled and chaotic, and headed towards the cash register with the bill.

When they entered the main dining room, the waitresses were all standing close to the exit and watching them. Their hostess pointed and the others covered their mouths. A siren could be heard coming closer.

"What's going on?" Felix asked to the emptying room, but no one answered. They were all filing out.

Dark faces appeared in the glass of the doorway, looking in. When they became clear, the bag full of electronics fell from Tomás' arms and he let out a curse. It was the faces of Earl and Smith, fully uniformed, looking in at them. When Smith caught sight of Felix standing there, a wide grin broke out across the officer's face.

Chapter *22*

The man's sign said, "Anything helps. Bless you."

The man didn't seem to notice Felix there, where he sat inside the dark glass of the Plymouth.

It might be his last chance.

So, Felix began yelling and smacking his head against the window. Softly at first, and then, realizing that his skull was at least as hard as the glass, with abandon.

"Help," he yelled, the handcuffs cutting into his wrists.

The man on the sidewalk lowered his sign and looked questioningly at the window. As Earl hit the gas, Smith stuck an arm over the seat and hit Felix full in the face with a stream of mace.

"That's for slashing the tires, cost me 200 bucks," Smith yelled.

His skin, his nose, his eyes, all of his pores and membranes revolted in one hateful moment. The pain was white hot and slimy, as if his skin had instantly undergone the worst of all sunburns. Mucus poured from his nose in a torrent and he found himself crying out, losing control of his senses.

The Plymouth merged and Earl was yelling. "Why would you shoot that shit off in the car you jackass, now it's everywhere. For fuck sake."

Both men in the front seat were coughing and retching, windows rolled down now and just barely keeping the vehicle moving between the lanes. Tomás was the only one not to cry out, but he grimaced in pain.

"A bomb threat. You guys are really, really unlucky, you know that?" Earl said.

Smith laughed, coughing in between chuckles. "That waitress was scared shitless. Took one look at your brown friend here and convinced herself that the Taliban had infiltrated the Piccadilly."

Now they were both laughing wildly, coughing between the big inhalations of breath.

"And then, finding that little sissy pistol in your pocket and pulling it out for everyone to see," Smith said at Felix. "You are lucky we didn't let that crowd at you. It wouldn't have been a nice way to go. Torn to shreds by little old ladies."

Felix, was fading in and out from the pain, he slumped over in his seat, fearing he would pass out. He couldn't see what was happening in the front seat now, his eyes nearly sealed closed, but he could hear the distinctive sound of Smith fiddling with the recording equipment.

"Let's just see what you guys dug up, shall we?"

And he played it.

"What is it?" Earl asked, zipping through the civilian traffic.

"It ain't good," Felix heard Smith saying, as he lost his fight for consciousness. "Looks like they might have had their last supper. Hope it was a good one fellas."

Sometime later he was jostled awake by a rough roadway. He opened his eyes, which still burned, but not too severely to see. The landscape had changed. The two-lane highway was elevated above saw palmettos and cypress knees. It was the swamp and Smith was on the phone.

"Yeah…Yeah…they got you on tape you know. We think it is time for the Segnette plan…Yeah…Yes…We'll take care of it."

So it's the swamp after all, Felix thought to himself, feeling the panic turning in his stomach.

"How to Dispose of a Corpse in Three Easy Steps."

"Louisiana Swampland: Your New Forever Home."

"Amateur Sleuth Sticks His Neck Out One Inch Too Far – You Won't Believe What Happens Next!"

"Oh, looks like he decided to wake up," Earl said from the driver's seat. "Just in time."

Felix still felt all but choked by the mucus, but the burning had sunk to a bearable level of torment. He looked over to Tomás, who leaned against the window with red, forlorn eyes.

The Plymouth bounced down a series of gravel roads and then, briefly, onto one of packed clay. *Could handcuffs be picked?* Felix had time to wonder, to dream. Could he get his feet under the chain, get his hands in front of him, and use the metal to choke out Smith in the passenger seat? He watched the bald head, speckled with cancerous looking sunspots, bob in front of him, and pictured smashing it like an egg. There had to be some way to smash it.

They came to rest on a green bit of earth between two great logs.

Earl killed the engine and they all sat there breathing for a minute, windows down. The car still reeked of capsaicin.

"Did you know that you have a police file down at the station Felix?" Earl asked. The officer leaned his buttock to the side and clipped the key to the Plymouth onto a small ring on his utility belt.

"A well-documented history of substance abuse," Smith put in, his fat face profiled in the ruddy light of the afternoon swamp.

Earl continued, his accent thickening. "It will also be noted that, laid low by the untimely death of your brother Robert, you fell to pieces. The drug use increased, to the point where you were experiencing hallucinations, seeing things that just weren't there. Delusions of grandeur, I reckon they'd call it, ideas about some great conspiracy concerning some of the city's most cherished residents."

"Illuminati shit," Smith put in, "wearing spaghetti strainers on your head. You know."

"Declaring to your most trusted friend and family servant, Tomás De…whatever, that you could no longer bear the overwhelming burden of your fraternal grief, you drove out here to the swamp, claiming that you were ready to 'end it all'. And then, once you'd reached the quiet hum of the swamp, entirely defeated by your loss, you flung yourself into the water."

"Even rich kids drown themselves. I'm sure you've read about it in a storybook or two," Smith said, sardonic and twisted.

"You'll have to shoot me," Felix said, "Someone will find my body and you'll end up in Angola for the rest of both your shit-eating lives."

Earl nodded. "That's just what your brother Robert said. Although he was a bit smoother around the edges than you are. What was it he said exactly?"

Smith looked up. "*This will not stand.* I think that was it."

"But it stood alright. Or knelt, if you'd prefer," Earl said with a little chuckle. He spit a long stream of tobacco juice out the window and into the grass. "But jackass here forgot to search him thoroughly enough, and that was how he ended up slipping that mask onto his head. Damn near gave us a heart attack with that one. But we won't make the same mistake twice. We are getting kinda good at this."

Smith had pulled out a small, black leather doc-kit from somewhere in the glove box. He laid it open in his lap, and Felix could just see the rows of bottles and syringes as the officer ran his fingers across them.

"And then Tomás as well. Old man went in trying to save his young friend, drowned in an attempted rescue."

Tomás opened his eyes and gave Smith a look that could wilt wildflowers. Smith ignored him and turned back towards Felix.

"A druggie like you is going to need a double dose I reckon."

With a long slow nod Smith plucked a bottle out of its little holster, shook it once, and twisted off the cap. Felix squinted to read the label, but his eyes were still stung from the mace, and he couldn't lock in on the wavering fine print. A syringe went into the bottle and filled up nearly to the top.

"You know, I really like a hit of this stuff sometimes, when the wife is out and I got the whole house to myself. Nothing wrong with getting a little high. The thing of it is, you become open to just about anything. Like being hypnotized almost. But that is only with a high enough dose. I remember one time I saw a commercial for Domino's, and I must have ordered about six pizzas. Decided to cut the dose after that."

Smith sprayed a tiny bit of the liquid into his mouth.

"Just a few drops to take the edge off, now in your case…"

And before Felix could react, the needle went through his pants and into the meat just above his knee.

It was at that moment that Tomás leaned forward, took a chunk of Smith's shoulder flesh between his teeth, and bit down as hard as he could.

Smith howled in pain. Earl pulled out his pistol and hit the old man over the head with it, once, twice, and nearly a third time before Tomás' jaw relaxed. Both officers got out of the car and opened Tomás' door. Earl grabbed the old man bodily, head-butted him, and threw him out into the mud.

Felix watched this scrape unfold in a stunned and heavy lull. He was aware of the Scopodol flowing through his veins. The drug rushed into his limbs with a warm familiarity and the opiate tinge of it was like a fireplace in winter, like a puppy in your lap, like a syrupy flame you could touch, all washing over him with a lambent glow. It was an old love letter found in a shoebox. The peppery hurt in his nose, eyes, mouth and heart started to soften almost immediately. While he'd been a great taker of pills for years, Felix had never had a potent inebriant directly injected into his body. He was amazed at the immediacy of it. A cloud settled over him. He watched his friend fall onto the swampy ground and felt peace. He looked at the man standing over Tomás with a gun in hand and his mind went awash with an easy sense of acceptance.

"The Short, Happy life of Felix Herbert," his mental headline read.

A soft, easy, friendly life. Adversarial nature may have had a brief episode here at the end, but for most of his years it had been a rubber-padded world. He was thankful for that. And, really, why be so scared of death? He couldn't remember the time before he was born as being particularly frightening. With any luck, death would be just the same. It would be nothing, not existing. A long walk in a wintry park.

Now he found himself outside of the car. A tow truck had pulled up behind the officers with a bearded man in the cab. Hitched to the truck was the Herbert family Continental.

"Is that our car?" Felix wondered aloud.

"Of course it is," Earl said cruelly. "How else would you drive out here to drown yourself? The helicopter is in the shop I guess."

Felix watched from a cloud as the men put Tomás in the driver's seat of the Plymouth and handcuffed him to the steering wheel, where he slumped over. As Felix was being led away, he could see Tomás just coming to, writhing in pain.

Felix trod on through the swamp and the world was taking on a swirling, devilish quality. The euphoria was fading and a dreamy sense of dissociation replaced it. Shapes appeared and then vanished in the shadows. Two men were behind him. That was all he knew.

The path ended in green water. A voice told him to kneel. He found himself doing so, a simpering wave of obedience overcoming him. His soul submitted.

"You just became drowned with sorrow and ruin," Earl bellowed, a hand raised up to his sermon. With his other hand he gestured towards the path they had come down, indicating to his partner.

Spanish moss twisted in the wind, lily pads curled like pained lips in the dark water just in front of Felix and in the deep there were eyes. Felix could see them, could look towards them for acceptance. He'd be joining them, a brother in whatever dark and infinite abyss lay under, down with Robert and all other men before and after.

Earl cleared his throat. "Distraught, you realized that you had no options left. No other course before you but this one."

Felix felt a pinch in his stomach, and then the tears came. The story was so sad, so short, so unfulfilled. But it was true, all of it. He felt it now in his bones. It was all his own fault.

"Powerless, afraid, and alone in a world that you were too sheltered to understand….you rushed along into a cowardly solution."

Sobs tore through Felix, his chest heaved in and out and he cried into the green water.

"And with the death of your brother, you began to lose your mind."

Felix felt a heavy weight pulling him towards the mire, a tiredness of all things, a stone around his neck that would never lift. Perhaps it was time.

He found himself crawling forward, towards the water.

They all heard it. A rumbling in the distance. The revving of a great beast— the sound of powerful combustion and undulating, pushing pistons throwing energy into four wheels that slurped as they spun in the mud.

Then, there was the Plymouth. It roared and the sunspots rolled over its dull black hood. It bore on with full force, twisting side to side in the quag as the city-soft tires lost and then regained their purchase.

Earl tugged at his belt buckle, swore, clearly forgetting the leather strap that kept his sidearm secured. Still the car bore on. Smith yelled something to his partner, who finally had the mechanism of his weapon unclasped and had his gun in his hand. In the split second before he was able to raise his weapon to the windshield, the front bumper of the car caught Earl by the hip. A loud thud echoed against the theatre of the cypress grove, and an animal groan croaked out of Earl as he tumbled aside, as loose-limbed as a child's doll. He twisted and floundered in the swampy shallows, crying out in pain.

The Plymouth barreled past, right into officer Smith. It hit him full on, with all of its force, and his body flew through the air like a ragdoll. He landed in a crook of cypress knees, his neck twisted in an unsettling position.

After hitting Smith, the driver engaged the brakes, but it was too late. There was no ABS on a car so dated, and the vehicle slid on and down, splashing into the swamp and throwing up a wave of foul-smelling sludge a few feet from where Felix knelt.

The sound it made was a flat thud, a belly flop of sheet metal. The vehicle bobbed a few times before it began to sink.

And then, in the haze and chaos of it all, Felix was vaguely aware of Tomás, his dear friend, sitting in the driver's seat of the Plymouth, now sinking. His dear, sweet Tomás, with green water rising up to his chest. He could hear the rattling of a chain, and the groans coming from officer Earl, who lay splashing in the muck.

"Felix!"

A deep heaviness in his limbs. A thin powder over the whole world. Was this death? Had he died?

"Felix. You must listen to me."

It was his dear old friend. It was Tomás. How he loved his dear old friend, respected him like a father, confided in him like a brother. But those intense eyes sank away. That cherished face receded into the swamp. It was saying something. Felix listened close.

"They handcuffed me to the steering wheel. The handcuff key is on the bald one. He looks dead. I think he broke his neck when he landed. Look, over there by the roots. Quickly. It is on his belt!"

Tomás was up to his neck now. The water around him was gurgling. The earth was sucking up the dark Plymouth, was devouring everything.

There was a dead man by some roots, a shiny key glimmering from his tool belt. Felix had to get the key. The key shone bright. One step forward now. Two steps.

Officer Earl groaned again, louder this time, he twisted around and began to speak muddled words.

Felix found the key on the dead man's belt, turned back to Tomás. It was past his chin now, the swamp, coming for him, rising up. It was an angry swamp. All of it roiled and bubbled. There were so many bubbles.

"Use the key Felix!"

His legs shook with each further step but they carried him to Tomás, whose mouth had now gone underwater. He handed the key to the drowning man and with a few desperate turns the cuffs came open. The old man wormed his way out of the window just as the roof of the Plymouth went under the surface of the water.

Officer Earl had sat up now and had his gun raised up in the air.

By the time Tomás had regained his feet, Earl had gripped his weapon properly and was attempting to aim it. It was clear that he was dazed. His shooting arm rotated in a tiny circle and he squeezed the trigger. The bullet splashed into the water, missing them by a few feet.

"RUN! Vámonos!" Tomás screamed.

The sun was setting. The two of them lunged out into the swamp.

And Felix ran, his hands held out in front of him and his vision swimming with terrors that rose, yellow-eyed, from among the roots— grim visions of the dead trembling in the dusk.

The sounds of a thousand frogs, the pat of splashing footfalls, and it was the darkest night. He felt a tug around his collar, by which Tomás pulled him onward, desperately urging him deeper into the marsh.

Chapter 23

"When they pulled me out of the car, I was able to snatch that Plymouth key from off his belt. I...I can't believe we are still alive, Felix."

But Felix didn't feel lucky. They had stopped for a moment to catch their breaths, leaning against tree trunks in the inky blackness. His legs felt leaden and his head spun with the chemical.

"Let's go...be very quiet," Tomás said, and on they ran. The tripping roots and molasses water made it hard to go with much speed. Felix felt more and more lost, waves of confusion washing over him. The running had upped his circulation, pushing the Scopodol through his blood with increasing vigor, pumping it wholesale into his brain. There was nothing else now. An old man. A dark swamp. A need to move forward forever— for some monster surely crept up from behind. He saw images of a sinking car, a crumpled man, a body under the wheels of a great locomotive thrusting its way through this dark. He saw Robert.

Life and death in a delicate balance. A few more yards, a few less, made all the difference. And yet he laughed.

Tomás tripped and caught himself against a fallen log. "You must be absolutely silent my dear boy. Our lives depend on it."

Felix nodded, all that was funny and light dissipating in an instant. He found himself lifting his friend up from the swamp ooze once again.

They stumbled on, Tomás turning his head to check that Felix was still following. Step after step the swamp deepened, fetid and charged with uncertainty. Impossible, now, to sense what was ahead, behind, above or below them. They were in a void. No light, no stars, only wet darkness and crickets, frogs in their millions.

Waist deep in the water, they froze. A loud splash, barely registered movement. Some large animal sliding off a log directly in front of them, ten feet away. Felix imagined it as some sort of spirit, but Tomás knew.

"An alligator, Felix. There was an alligator. We nearly walked into him."

They stopped, letting the fear cool for a moment. The old man bent a willow sapling back and forth until he had a stick five feet long. With it he beat the surface of the water in front of him, making a quiet splash every time they entered a new grove.

Felix followed the slapping rhythm of the stick, imagining it as the sound the bullet makes when it finds a fat part of the human body: driving away what lurks beneath in an instant.

They stopped again after another ten minutes of slogging through the muck.

"There! I can see headlights. This must be a road," Tomás said, his voice cracking with joy. He held a hand up for stillness, and the two of them waited while the light faded and obscured. Then they crept on.

The land sloped upward abruptly, the palmetto fronds fading into state-sown St. Augustine, and then into blacktop. Tomás stopped and wrung out the cuffs of his pants. He took off his black shoes and threw them forcefully back into the darkness of the swamp. Then he turned and looked at his young charge. Felix was bleeding from thorns he had forced his way through.

"Felix? Are you alright my boy?"

"I may die."

"We are alive yet Felix. I imagine that redneck cop will have no luck finding us now, his car stuck in the mud. Although…he could take our car. Though it might ruin his plan. I think it best to follow this road until we find a car, a house, a shop. Anywhere with a telephone. And then we call Melancon straight away."

They smiled and embraced each other, patting each other's moist backs before choosing a direction, each thanking whatever spirit had seen them through the ordeal.

But they were premature in their sighs of relief. For someone had heard them, seen them come crawling out of the quag, and it was no spirit.

Felix pointed towards the white Escalade a moment before its lights went on. He had sensed it there, a dark and unbreathing thing lying in wait. It now came to life with high beams pointed in their direction. Tomás recoiled and pulled Felix back towards the darkness of the swamp.

But it was too late. The tank-like machine rolled up alongside them and a thin hand extended from the driver's window, pointed a pistol towards the sky and fired a shot that caused both men to freeze in place.

Then the car door opened and Lena Troxclair stepped out into the night.

She looked ill-prepared for swamp life wearing pumps and a white dress, as if she'd just come from another ball. Her face was twisted— Felix could just see it in the headlights, the eclipse of the hunchback shining around the edges, a lambent hill rising out of the mire. She stepped towards them.

Was she smiling? Or was it anger?

"So we come to this," she said. They watched her move closer.

"You ever go to church Felix?" She was yelling now, to be audible over the chorus of chirping frogs.

He felt Tomás' hand on his shoulder. "What?" he yelled back.

"I asked if you'd ever been to church."

They could see the glint of the pistol in the headlights now. There was nothing to do but answer.

"No."

Her silhouette nodded. "I didn't think so. And why not?"

He paused, struggling to think clearly. "I never thought God was going to help me any."

"Smart boy."

"But Robert went," Tomás yelled at her. "He went before you murdered him."

She paced in front of the headlights and her dress sparkled.

"Up there where I'm from, Felix, those little country churches, they teach you it is all about *acceptance*. About, your *role* in life. We are all given a special *purpose* for our existence. It's handed down from on high. Delivered from the scripture, from the hand of God himself."

She moved faster, stomping on the asphalt in her pointed heels.

"And we humans, we have no say in any of that. You know? And here I am a woman. A little girl born up there into nothing. And my role is *this*, and your *role* is that, and on and on and on."

"You're the victim here?" Tomás yelled at her.

Felix was coming down, the world regaining its sharp edges. The drug had all but faded.

She shook her head, ignoring Tomás. "And to justify it all, they teach you a bunch of bullshit about the nature of mankind. How we were created out of rib bones and good intentions. Souls, spirits, made in His image. All of that."

He blinked his eyes. He could see her face now in the night. Lena was crying.

"But here you are Felix. Look at you. You know, it never ceases to amaze me. The science behind it all. I learned when I left that goddamned church. Just how much is determined by one's genetics. How much we really are still slaves, and how our roles really *are* determined by things we just can't control. That is why. That is why all of this. You are just a younger, less successful version of Robert, after all."

Felix could hear everything clearly now. Was that the sound of the hammer being pulled back on the revolver, heard over the roaring swamp? Whether real or imagined, that sound shook him awake, sobered him in one instant.

Lena continued. "A load of feel good horse shit. That's right, you *can't* be whatever you want to be. You can only be who the fuck you are." She let out a sobbing, hysterical peal of laughter.

"God it feels good to fucking curse. Jesus fucking Christ. You should see the kind of people I was with an hour ago. It's like there is a gene for being an uptight, pretentious fuck as well."

"Listen…" Felix began, but the woman was rising to something, and talked over him just as she had the frogs.

"No. The real truth is that you are born into who you are, into exactly who you are going to be. No matter how much you try to fight it. There is no escape from it. And you Felix, you are a perfect fucking example of what I'm talking about. Nature over nurture, over God, over it all. You are just a series of fucking brain chemicals. I mean you were born rich, right? And your brother Robert, may he rest in fucking peace, was born poor."

She paused for a moment, nodding her head. "Oh yeah, I know a whole lot about you and your family Felix. Don't act as if you are surprised. I know you found my camera. What you never found were the dozen other eyes and ears we've had on your family for the past year. All the people I have, poring over every detail about the Herberts. Because that is what money can buy, Felix. That's what you don't realize yet, for all your family's riches."

The gun was pointed at his chest, accusatory. The bit of lead inside waited to fall into his flesh. Where would it strike? Would it be one shot or multiple? A simple heavy feeling before lights went out? Or prolonged gasping as the blood pooled in his lungs? Felix's thoughts turned to the morbid details of what he was about to go through.

Lena kept on. "I know about your batshit crazy old man and about your boozy ruinous mother, about your pill popping and your failures to live up to the family name. Your ratty apartment and dead-head job you took to try and, I don't know, drum up some sense of purpose for yourself? By, what, chopping tomatoes? You fucking men are pathetic."

"You don't know anything about me," Felix let out.

She feigned offense, waving the gun barrel in a small circular motion.

"Listen kid, I know it all. I had to claw my way down here, to hustle every second of my life to escape that fucking church, to get out of the role that was handed down to me. But here I am, I made my own purpose. And I still can't escape the responsibility of cleaning up shit after you men are done fucking it all up."

"You're insane," Felix said.

She scoffed. "And you? What have you got to show for your life? You know what? It doesn't matter what you've done in the past month. The fact of the matter is, at the end of the day, you are just the same as your brother Robert. The inability to just let things fucking go, it runs in your family. And now it has gotten you killed."

"She's not insane, she's just evil," Tomás yelled. "God is listening to you woman. He is seeing what you do here tonight."

That seemed to make her laugh. "That's it? That's your argument? Your final words?"

"Why did you kill my brother?" Felix asked.

She nodded her head. "Your family is rich Felix, but you are the new rich. There is no shame in it. I'm the new rich too. The fact of the matter is that with Scopodol Robert could have made your family go from rich to actually *wealthy*. Do you understand that distinction Felix? I doubt that you do.

But you could have known what wealth everlasting was like, and so could have Robert. With the Krewe all put together I had a virtual ATM. A simple cocktail really. Take a room full of liquored up, networking doctors, thrust together, wearing masks, all part of a tribe. Do you know how much money a pharm rep will pay for an invitation to such an event? To be able to ply their wares? To be a part of the Krewe I created out of an old boys club? But because both you and your brother seem to have some genetic inability to let shit slide, to leave well enough alone, it was all about to be ruined. Robert had to start in with the 'code of ethics' nonsense. The calls to the FDA. Turning away all that cash from the people at Halcyon.."

"So you're a drug pusher *and* a murderer," Felix said.

"There it is again, that ridiculous sense of fairness. But let me tell you a little secret that would have saved Robert's life: There is no such thing as *just deserts*. I've gotten this far haven't I? I'll figure it out Felix. Because you are in my way, just like Robert was. My whole life asshats like you two have tried to throw up walls to block me in, and I've smashed through them every time. Just like I'm going to do now."

The barrel of the pistol went still. The frogs hushed. The world went slow and syrupy around him.

"At least you've found your purpose at last Felix. To die here in the swamp with an old man you have to *pay* to be your friend."

She put both hands on the pistol now, ready for the recoil, the barrel pointed just at his heart. And in that black hole at the end of the revolver, Felix could sense eternity.

He couldn't help but smile. He couldn't help but see the headlines.

"Greenhorn Goes to Grave Grinning."

"Determined Dick Dies with Dignity."

"Smiling Sleuth Shot in Swamp."

Felix looked at Lena. "You can't kill everyone in the world with a conscience."

"That's a poor person's attitude, Felix. Can't win so don't try?"

She walked towards him and he could see that she was shaking. Tears still glistened in her eyes. Her gait was unsteady and her face was tight. And he could see other things as well.

Far off in the distance, down the swamp road inestimable miles and miles, Felix saw a light then— a pinprick in the black skin of the night. For a second, he imagined that he was already dead, and that what he was witnessing was nothing more than the light at the end of the long tunnel, hope at the end of so much suffering.

Had she really failed to notice it? Failed to see the bright light, no, now two bright lights steadily coming towards their little scene? Felix stood waiting for her to pull the trigger.

And she did.

Chapter 24

Until this point, she had killed only with words. Humans at least. Growing up in the country, she'd killed all of the following first hand: extra kittens, fryer chickens, nuisance raccoons, and once a deer. Even so, the true nature of murder remained somewhat abstract to her. For so long she'd had others doing the deed for her. Acting out her will. But that's not to say she wouldn't. In fact, she had dreamed about it with some longing. To kill a man was surely one of the most exhilarating experiences a person could have. A feeling of power, to take a life. No more feeling weak, or walked on, or held up. It would be pure ecstasy.

Saving lives, that was something she had done plenty of. But it never felt fully satisfying. Not like it was supposed to be. Doctors always talked about it, mostly the men, as if putting people back together, letting them go on with their boring lives, was some kind of God-like power. They really saw themselves that way, sometimes. Little Gods of the OR. But in her mind, she might as well have been a clock maker. Set that bone, give that shot, remove that tumor. Send them on their way back to their television sets.

She was familiar with death, also, was familiar with the capricious and cruel way that kinetics often dealt with the human form. She pictured it now. The path the bullet would take through the thick air. The explosion of blood. She was working up to it. She was ready to see her will through, to end all of this nonsense and go back to pulling her way up the ladder any way she could. She was almost there now. Almost untouchable.

She aimed. She squeezed, but not quite hard enough. The resistance of the trigger surprised her. The gun in her hands moved forward just slightly and she tensed up in the horrible, thrilling moment. This was not like a chicken. Her eyes closed. And then she fired. She fired at what she thought was the heart of Felix Herbert. The gun spit wickedly in her hand and her ears sang out in a piercing wail.

The blast. The smoke. The fire. The sick elation at what she'd done.

Lena lowered the gun. Felix crumpled. The old Latin man stood over him moaning. She raised the gun again. No mistakes this time. It's just a kind of surgery. She felt her heart beating. The old man had turned towards her. What was he looking at? What was that light in his eyes?

She turned.

Behind her two pinpricks of light were waxing, fully forming into two headlights now, attached to some sort of a car.

"Shit, shit, shit."

It pulled behind her, about a hundred feet away, and she turned to face it. Hopefully it was Earl and Smith, finally come to make this cleanup job easy on her. They would do the work that she was struggling to do. Her whole body shook now.

Felix still hadn't made a sound, but his feet were kicking the grass near the roadside. The butler was no longer there. She looked for him in the darkness until she heard the squeak of a car door opening.

She put her gun hand up to her brow. The lights were too bright. It was hard to make out. There was a man in a hat standing there. Lena squinted, long tear streaks winding down through her makeup, mascara blotted on her flesh like a pox, and her hunchback quivered with uncertainty. She swung the gun on the new arrival, not recognizing the shape of the man.

"The jig is up Lena," the new man shouted.

It was the Detective. Melancon, was it? People were always putting walls in her path. Always men. She should have done this old one in when he was passed out unconscious in her guest bedroom. What would have been easy then would be difficult out here in the swamp. Three bodies now. She'd have plenty of thoughtful cleanup to do after this. But for now, she'd have to be rough, fearless. She steadied her breath. Her heart was beating too fast. She thought of blood. It was all that mattered now.

"I shot a man," she screamed at Melancon, equal parts glee and Sunday confession. "And I can do it again. I'll empty this fucking thing right into your chest if you don't put your fucking hands up right now where I can see them. And turn those damn beams off!"

There was a long period of torpor. The headlights cast everything in dramatic stage light. The sounds of the nighttime swamp swelled to cacophony, and finally Melancon answered.

"You have to give it up sister. This is the end of the line. How many more life sentences do you want to tag on? I've got a gun too and I'm willing to bet I'm a better shot than you. Now, we can go to shooting bullets at each other and both end up with our insides tore to pieces, slowly dying out here in a swamp, or you can realize the jig is up. We know about the drug. We know everything."

She laughed. Whatever he thought he knew, it wasn't half of what she was into. The swim from backwater chawbacon to wealthy doctor hadn't been made with gentle, cautious strokes. Not at all.

"You've got to be kidding me. Don't you have anything better to do with your time? In this city, of all places. Shouldn't you have plenty of people to chase after without getting in my way? I've never hurt a single person without them asking for it pretty clearly first detective. And what I see right now is you asking for it. So I'll give you one last chance to get back in your piece of shit car and drive away."

"That's not happening," Melancon said.

Did he have his gun drawn? It was hard to see in the blinding light. He was holding something over the door of his car. It must be a gun. She would have only one chance, and it had to be perfect, deadly. It had to finish him.

But just as she was about to take that chance, she felt a thud on the back of her head and her knees buckled underneath her. The world spun for a second and she found the ground rushing up to meet her.

Chapter *25*

He had space and time. The pain that shot through his back, the horror of seeing Felix shot, the memories he had— these things would not stop Tomás De Valencia. Not this night. Honor was more important than fear, after all, and acting brave was being brave despite all the terror and doubt he felt in that swampy, black night.

Her back was turned; her eyes and pistol were locked onto the detective. The headlights cast everything in an evil glow. They were yelling at each other, fully engaged, and here was a chance at something. A moment to rise to greatness. He looked down at Felix, where he lay on the grass. Tomás De Valencia was not a doctor, but he could see that the wound might not be a kill-shot. At least he hoped. And prayed. He still believed that God would help him. But first he had to help himself.

He looked at Felix a last time. The bullet had gone in the shoulder and looked to have come out the other side. But he couldn't be sure. It was dark and black. The blood was black. It flowed out of the young man, out of his friend, out of his love. In the night's blackness De Valencia could see the face of his long dead brother, Eme, looking up at him with Felix's eyes.

"Don't be afraid, my boy, courage now," he said.

Felix nodded. There was life left in him. If only Tomás De Valencia could rise to this moment, things might be set right in one fiery spell of daring.

And so, Tomás De Valencia disappeared into that swamp-black night.

Here he was in a moment of separation, stalking through the cypress trees, circling around until he was close to her. Now he could make out some words, see the detective clearly in profile, the glinting pistols aimed at each other.

Tomás De Valencia would make this right. He would swing away. If he could only straighten his back, unruffle himself, act with confidence and do a thing that he had never before brought himself to do.

His fingers wrapped around the base of the branch and drug it forward. It was wet, slimy, slick; but it was heavy. He stood and turned. Now he too was nearly blinded by the headlights, but not entirely. He lifted it up fully out of the water. The heft of the wood felt pleasant in his hands and he curled his socked foot in the St. Augustine, trying his best to be a leaf, a stick, a thing of the swamp that she needn't turn to scrutinize.

He inched closer. She cursed and spat towards the light and her hunch bobbed in fury.

One step closer, then another. As he was nearly within striking distance Tomás De Valencia let out a long groan as he brought the weight of the branch down on the back of her head.

In that moment, he thought of Eme.

She sighed and stumbled forward. She seemed to be hesitating on which direction she would shoot. The pistol flailed as she went to her knees. A splash of black blood was visible on her haunch.

Her face went angry as she fired, crumpling to the ground.

The sound of shattering glass tore through the night and one of Melancon's headlights went dark.

The detective rushed at her, pistol pointed downwards. She writhed a bit, rolling on her hunch like a beetle on its back. Her eyes were tight. Tomás De Valencia stood over her, triumphant.

"Shit man, you were really batting for the fences there." The detective bent down and took the pistol from where it rested on the pavement alongside Lena Troxclair.

Tomás De Valencia rushed over to be with his friend.

"How are you feeling Felix?"

He smiled, showed his teeth, rocked from side to side there grinning.

"It hurts to be shot."

"You are going to be just fine," Tomás De Valencia promised his young friend, already tearing pieces of his clothing off and using them to wrap the wound in Felix's shoulder, hoping to still the bleeding.

"Do you think I'll die?"

Melancon shook his head. "No kid. You are going to be fine. Probably not going to have a professional sports career, or anything like that, but you'll live."

"Do you know how to stop the bleeding?" Tomás asked the detective.

A few blinks in the night. "Well, shit, the only doctor here is knocked out cold. Thanks to you."

"Goddamn it man. Call an ambulance or something."

After a moment of confusion, Melancon managed to work his aging flip phone away from his trouser clip. He punched in a few numbers and was pacing over Lena, trying to give a dispatcher directions to their location. Tomás De Valencia also kept a cold eye on the witch where she lay in the single spotlight of the El Camino.

Tomás stared up at the stars and felt his fingers twitching at the end of his arm. It was the first time he'd purposefully hurt another human being. Well, aside from punching Felix, but he could hardly remember that as being purposeful anyway. He didn't feel guilty about Lena though. He was glad. Joyous like he would never have imagined.

The boy was stammering out something on the grass, and Tomás leaned over him.

Off in the darkness, the detective was screaming at the emergency dispatcher. "Of course there is no address, we are on the highway, in the swamp. Yes. Yes. I don't know. Yes. OK. Please hurry."

"How did you find us man?" Felix spurted out, after the detective had finished his call. Melancon bent over him.

"Your Mother called me. Said both of you were missing after going to Lena's office. I had a tracker on the Plymouth. Found it half sunk in the drink about a mile from here. Figured I'd keep going and see if there was any other sign. I guess that was the right move."

The young man smiled and tried to writhe onto his side.

"No, you just stay still now."

In his turning, Felix cast his eyes out into the abyss of the swamp. Tomás noticed a change come over the boy then. The pain went out of his face. Something else lit up his eyes.

The detective and Tomás were both bent low. The boy seemed to be trying to tell them something, but couldn't. His voice came out raspy, muffled. They couldn't hear him now over the swamp sounds.

With his good hand, Felix grabbed the gun where it was resting untethered in Melancon's holster. The detective seemed too shocked to react in time. He moved to put his hand out, but the young man had already let loose with a shot that forced both the detective and Tomás to instinctively fall backwards, away from the blast. In the moment that

235

followed two more shots went out into the blackness behind them.

They all heard it then in the ringing silence that followed: a moan and a splash.

Tomás De Valencia moved forward towards his friend, unsure what had happened. There was a loud ringing in his ears, but he put a hand on the boy's shoulder and shook him gently. Felix had gone limp, only passed out Tomás hoped, and now lay with his good arm out to his side, still gripping the pistol.

"Christ," Melancon said. He had frozen in place, his backside in the damp grass.

After he'd collected himself, the detective stood and produced a small flashlight. Walking over to the edge of the swamp, they found officer Earl, his lips puckered out in horror. Two of the three shots had hit him in the chest.

"How the hell did Felix see him?" the detective asked, incredulous.

But Tomás De Valencia only smiled.

Nearly forty-five minutes later, the helicopter flew in low, its bright beam of light stroking the tips of the cypress trees as it sputtered through the fog. Melancon and Tomás De Valencia watched it together. The ambulances arrived soon after, along with a dozen or so officers.

They were smart people, reckoned Tomás. Most of them were smart enough to not start asking too many questions, not yet. They all knew how many questions would come later, and how closely everything they did at this moment would be scrutinized. They looked from the detective, to the broken young man, to the floating police corpse off in the swamp, and finally to the handcuffed, well dressed woman squirming in the roadway.

They looked at all of that, Tomás reckoned, and wisely said as little as possible.

But they did give Tomás De Valencia and the detective some coffee, positioned them on the tailgate of one of the giant police pickup trucks with the intimidating brush guards, and told them just to, "take it easy."

Felix they put in an ambulance. Tomás De Valencia, though he insisted with the use of a few expletives, was not allowed to join him.

Chapter *26*

He'd been winged by a hollow-point, an approximately .357 inch diameter lump of lead. The hot metal tore through his right shoulder where it opened in a wicked blossom, burst through his clavicle (which absorbed enough of its force to break into 28 separate pieces), rived a few nerve endings, and then exited out through his back with an eruption of blood, bone, and tissue. He'd lost three pints of blood, and could no longer make a fist with his right hand.

It was a rainy day, but Felix took the streetcar anyway. It was good to sit in that old metal thing: open to the air, clanging its way down the Avenue, filled with people. He sat in the very back, helping himself to the reversed handicapped seat. Was it still the handicapped seat? Before every chair in the car was turned to head the opposite direction and the driver went to the butt end for his return trip? He wasn't really handicapped, was he? But his entire right side was in a cast. A removable cast, with its network of straps and noisy Velcro clasps. The car jostled and bounced, which hurt his arm, but he didn't mind. Spring was coming— it was now Lent, the city austere and sober and ready in the morning light.

He disembarked near Tulane Medical Center, where he had PT three times a week to regain full motor control of his arm. Doctors said it would never work the same, but that didn't bother Felix. Doctors didn't know everything.

Of course, he'd had to take painkillers again, but he was careful to use them sparingly, and was now at a point where whole days would elapse with the little orange bottles sitting untouched in the cabinet. It wasn't the same anymore. There was no euphoria, only a heavy feeling and bad memories, a feeling of wasted potential. He was almost ready to flush the rest of what he had. Though the pain was bad, he knew he'd be able to bear it. He'd born more than he ever thought he could and come out in one piece.

He was enjoying his therapy; finding joy in the purpose and meaning of it. He learned to relish that feeling of steady, incremental progress, strength returning. It was an hour of gripping shapes, twisting bars, pulling levers, manipulation, all while one of a handful of good looking, competent therapists doted on him. All four of them were young women, positive, peppy. Depressed or somber people never seemed to become physical therapists. *Thank God*, he thought.

Spending time with them reminded him of how much happiness there still was out in the world, only waiting for him to grab it in his hand, to squeeze it like a grip trainer. He thought about which one of the women he liked best.

But right at that moment on the streetcar, he had other, bigger things still on his mind.

He met Tomás at a coffee shop near St. Patrick's church. There was a wedding on: the bride and groom pummeled with bird seed, the ringing of the bell. They watched the lovers climb into the back of the limousine and disappear down the street, leaving their friends and family behind to stand awkwardly on the church steps.

"You too, maybe. Perhaps soon you will start your own family?" Tomás asked over his coffee.

"Got to take care of myself, first."

The coffee was good and the weather was cold, but they sat outside anyway. They dodged around the trying details held by the next few hours, in which they would be cross examined by a team of attorneys defending Lena Troxclair on a whole slew of charges. For now though, they talked about happy things. Tomás had finally booked that trip back home, back to Guatemala for nearly a whole month of old friends and family dinners.

"You are sure you won't join me?"

"Sounds like something you've probably got to do alone. But I'll be down there any time you need me."

The old man rubbed his face and looked at the birds, brought in great nebulae now by all the wedding seed. He seemed to be gone already.

The trial was entering its second week. He knew there would be appeals as well: a second, third rehashing. The Troxclairs, of course, had the best lawyers money could buy, but it was clear that she was going to be locked up for years, even in the most generous sentencing. Felix had his own lawyer now, a chubby little Kentuckian who explained, with great detail, how the DA was salivating at the chance to make an example of Lena.

The room was stuffy, the mouthpieces cautious, soft-spoken. It was not the high courtroom drama that Felix might have envisioned. It was his third time giving testimony, and each time it was full of the same repeated questions, over and over again.

Yes, officer Smith had injected him with a drug he believed was Scopodol. No he wasn't a doctor. Well, he knew it was Scopodol because they told him it was and it was written on the damn bottle. Yes, Tomás had stolen the car key off of his belt as they tussled outside the car. Yes, Tomás had killed Smith with the Plymouth. Yes, he'd sunk into the swamp, handcuffed to the steering wheel. Then he'd clubbed Lena, and Felix had shot Earl, and so on. It was beginning to lose all its emotional power over him through the sheer repetition.

It went on and on in such a way. Lena sat slumped in her business clothes, but she was sleeping in jail at night, as her disheveled hair and raccoon eyes gave testimony. Bail had been set at fifty million, her assets frozen, her books turned over to the feds. She was a slumping, wheezing shell of a woman there in the courtroom, and if she had ever taken a notion to meet Felix's glare (she did not), he wouldn't have been the first to look away. He swore it to himself. He was no longer just *acting* brave. The fear in his heart was gone.

The *hate*, that he was working on. He'd stopped himself short of forgiving her, particularly when he'd heard all the details, as they came out, bit by bit in court.

Weeks later, at home with his mom and dad, he would tell the story he'd pieced together as best he could, after asking her first if she felt quite ready to hear it.

Six months before his death, Robert had attended a medical conference in town. It was there he met Lena Troxclair, who explained to him that she was trying to revive an old Mardi Gras Krewe exclusively for people in the medical profession. Robert loved the idea, of course, and according to the testimony of a few other club members, he had been responsible for much of the work that went into getting the Krewe organized.

It got a little hazy here, as the two men who had testified seemed to be only casual, tangential members, and couldn't speak at length on all the inner workings. Max Troxclair, using something called "Spousal Privilege," could not be compelled to testify about anything but the murder itself. But the gist of it was just as Felix had expected.

Robert was interested in the Krewe from a social perspective: fun, parties, relationships, a chance to form camaraderie. He organized a picnic, drinks, a night of clumsy bowling. Lena, according to the testimony of one Pharmaceutical Rep, had used the Krewe to generate money making opportunities.

There were gaps in the story here, holes that Felix had to fill himself, but thinking deeply on it he could already convince himself of what had happened. Robert had objected to Lena. Had it been a general objection, or a problem with the specific drug Scopodol, Felix would have to guess. What was for certain is that Robert placed calls, three weeks before his death, to both Halcyon Pharmaceuticals and to the FDA. He hadn't heard the one to the FDA, but the complaint to the company was specific, formal, and recorded. Robert had particular misgivings about the drug Scopodol. They had played the recording in court, in which Robert said that other doctors he knew were over-prescribing it, and that he was worried about the side effects: the memory loss, the suggestibility, the moral implications of losing one's will.

It had been good hearing his brother's voice again, another giant nail in the coffin of Lena Troxclair.

As for the actual fact of the matter: how Robert had been brought to his knees before a speeding train, and who had done the actual deed and how, seemed to be something that they were building up to.

But Felix knew. And he sat quietly in the courtroom with that knowing, just as he would the rest of his life.

But in court it was a slow process to bring that truth out. It was as if they wanted to soak up all the details first, to find out who Lena Troxclair and the two dead policemen had been. But he was waiting for that grand moment— Felix had his testimony all prepared, and transcribed the confessions of Earl and Smith as best as he was able to do from his cloudy memory, with corroboration from Tomás De Valencia of course.

Time passed. Tomás was excused by the court and by Felix's mother, and flew off to Guatemala.

While Tomás was gone, Felix met his mother one day actually vacuuming the house. He decided something had changed in her.

"I think we should fire Tomás," she said, when he asked her about it. Felix was horrified at first, until she made her intentions clear.

"I think we should fire him, but support him in his old age. He can live here with us as a family friend, and we will take care of him instead of the other way around. What do you think about that Felix?"

He'd have to think about it. He'd read too many stories of old people going to seed once their work was done.

"Let's ask him what he thinks about it when he gets back."

A week passed and then another. The case against Lena Troxclair was wrapping up. He'd pass by Melancon in the corridor of the courthouse and the old man would wink at him. The two were not supposed to talk to each other about the case, which would have been impossible, so for a while they simply didn't talk at all.

And then, just like that, Lena was found guilty of conspiracy to murder, along with sundry other crimes. She was given a life sentence. There were no tears in her eyes when they led her out of the courtroom. Felix had been there for it all.

It was late summer by the time he was truly ready to move on with his life, to find whatever it was that might come next.

On one day as the leaves were beginning to fall, Felix decided to visit Robert's grave, to give him the good news about justice being served.

The daily showers had already passed, but the graveyard drained poorly. Pools rose to the lips of stone mausoleum as Felix picked his way down the cement path, abandoning any care for his fine shoes as they became caked in the mud.

He arrived at Herbert family tomb through muscle memory.

He stopped when he saw the name, lately etched into marble. Fresh flowers were left there— Robert's wife Angelica, his children maybe. They seemed so far away, and yet here were the petals of their memory and hurt moldering in the heat.

Perhaps he'd been selfish, and now in this quiet yard, the countless dead weighed on him. Their regrets, their goals, their things left undone. The dead were legion.

He knelt at the grave of his older brother Robert.

"I'm sorry that I let you down so much in life Robert. I know I was a disappointment sometimes and that you never showed it. You were an honorable man and I wasn't. I didn't know how to be, you know? I think growing up rich is enough to ruin a person sometimes. You and Pop were so strong and competent, I guess I felt like it didn't matter whether I tried or not. But losing a brother... well, it is too early to say but I'm thinking that it changed me. It moved me to another end of the spectrum I guess. But it's a small comfort…compared to knowing I'll never have you back."

The wind blew a quiet answer and Felix smelled the warm air.

"I knew you wouldn't kill yourself. Wouldn't just call down the curtains on your whole family like that. You were no coward. You were the type that everyone could depend on, the type who kept his promises. I just hope that you might think the same of me now."

Footsteps.

Felix turned his head slowly.

"I know I'm interrupting Felix, but your Mom told me I'd find you here."

It was detective Melancon, hat in one hand, a bouquet of flowers in the other.

Felix turned back towards his brother. "Doesn't matter. I have all the time in the world to say all the things I want to say. The rest of my life. I don't have to say anything in a hurry."

"That's true."

He waited until Felix Stood up.

"I know your brother would be proud of you Felix."

Felix brushed the bits of gravel off of his pants legs, turning to face the detective.

"You really missed me that much?"

Melancon laughed and then, looking around at the tombs, cut himself short.

"Not an entirely social visit, son."

Felix took a moment to scan the city of the dead around him, weighing their silence.

"Well?"

"Well, for starters, I need to apologize. I didn't take you too seriously at first. The rich kid, chip on his shoulder, devastated by a big loss. I figured having something to prove was mixing in with all your grief and making you...well... temporarily insane. But it turns out maybe I'm not always correct. It turns out nearly every hunch you had was right on the money."

A bluebird landed on the corner of the Herbert tomb and Felix watched it peck at the moss and dead leaves in the gutters of the little building.

"So here is some news. It turns out that Scopodol is being rescheduled. All because of your brother and his sacrifice. People won't have to go through that anymore."

"Yeah, Robert took medicine seriously."

"Also, something you might not know. Max Troxclair has been under investigation this whole time, we are building a case on him that is looking pretty damning. The more we dig the more stuff comes to light. It really is turning out to be a rather large conspiracy. And it is all thanks to you. You blew this thing wide open Felix. You're going to have a dozen doctors in the clink before it's over with."

"Doesn't do any good now anyway," Felix said, gesturing towards his brother's grave.

"But it could. It could do some good Felix."

The detective took a few steps forward and gently placed the flowers on the steps leading up to the mausoleum gate. He put his hat back on his head and straightened his bowtie.

Felix smiled at him. He liked the detective, the candor of him, the stumbling mulishness, the direct and brash way he conducted himself. There were no lies in him.

Melancon looked him in the eye. "You know, all this corruption in the NOPD, what with those two bad apples you did away with, and everything else. Well, it has got me thinking, thinking maybe I'd like to go into business for myself. I know I've still got a few good years left in me."

"You mean like a private investigator?"

"That's right Felix. The thing is, I'm starting to get pretty old. And when a man gets as old as me, he needs help. Help from someone with a good head on his shoulders. Someone perceptive and energetic and with the gumption to take on all the evil in the world. Someone who is willing to fight. Someone who is brave."

A heavy silence hung amongst the graves.

"Felix. I'm saying if you aren't too busy chopping onions," Melancon said, extending his hand. "I think I could use a guy like you to help me."

Felix felt the warm thump of blood in his veins, and under the lonely watch of the dead and gone, he put the palm of his hand into Detective Melancon's, and gripped it tightly.

"Lost Soul Finds Purpose," his headline now read.

A Note from the Author:

Only **you** can solve Herbert and Melancon's next big mystery.

You've finished "The Krewe," and I hope you've enjoyed it. I put a lot of hours into making it the best reader experience possible, and I hope that came across in the words. As a small-time indie writer, those hours spent have to be budgeted out of a real life in which I spend forty plus hours a week running a business...all to put the roof in my stomach and the bacon over my head...how does that go again?

The point is (you probably guessed it), this is the part where I ask you for a **review**!

You see, as an indie writer, I am made or broken by exposure. If I get exposure, in the form of reviews, word of mouth, Goodreads lists, Twitter posts - or whatever else has lots of avid readers looking and talking - it means I'm able to succeed.

That publishing success, in turn, means I'm able to whittle away a few more hours from my business demands in order to write more words for you. Which is what I desperately want.

I hope that is what you want too.

So please, let the world know if you enjoy my work. The more you do that, the faster Felix and Melancon can get to the bottom of their next crazy, deadly, intriguing, New Orleans-y adventure!

They are both counting on you, dear reader. And so am I!

Please leave a review – Amazon, Goodreads, Facebook, Reddit, Twitter – whatever! You can also sign up for my mailing list at my blog: https://sethpevey.com/, for future updates, giveaways, and possibly even advanced beta-reader status!

Help Herbert and Melancon keep letting the good times roll!